Krishna
A Love Story

Ashis Gupta

BAYEUX

KRISHNA: A LOVE STORY
Copyright © 2007 Ashis Gupta

Cover Image: "Ganesh Janani" by Jamini Roy. Photography: Alexandra Kelko. From the private collection of Gautam and Manu Chakravartty, Hawaii, with permission.
Book design: Fiona Staples

Published by: Bayeux Arts, Inc., 119 Stratton Crescent SW, Calgary, Canada T3H 1T7, www.bayeux.com

Library and Archives Canada Cataloguing in Publication

Gupta, Ashis, 1940-
    Krishna : a love story / Ashis Gupta.
ISBN 978-1-896209-83-8
    I. Title.
PS8613.U68K74 2007   C813'.6   C2007-904418-2

First Printing: October 2007
Printed in Canada

> *Books published by Bayeux Arts/Gondolier are available at special quantity discounts to use as premiums and sales promotions, or for use in corporate training programs. For more information, please write to Special Sales, Bayeux Arts, Inc., 119 Stratton Crescent SW, Calgary, Canada T3H 1T7.*

All rights reserved. No part of this publication may be reproduced, stored in a retrieval system, or transmitted, in any form or by any means, electronic, mechanical, recording, or otherwise, without the prior written permission of the publisher, except in the case of a reviewer, who may quote brief passages in a review to print in a magazine or newspaper, or broadcast on radio or television. In the case of photocopying or other reprographic copying, users must obtain a license from the Canadian Copyright Licensing Agency.

The publishing activities of Bayeux/Gondolier are supported by the Canada Council for the Arts, the Alberta Foundation for the Arts, and by the Government of Canada through its Book Publishing Industry Development Program.

Dedicated to my mother, who instructed me in the love of books, and my father, who helped heal the body and fire the imagination

One

AND the hibiscus tree bloomed massive yellow flowers month after month, year after year, flowering day after day in such profusion as if its very existence depended on this ceaseless act of creation. Krishna spent hours looking out through the large glass drawing room window, oblivious of the traffic on the road in front of her house, unmindful of household chores that remained neglected. Crows landed on the lawn from time to time, stray dogs wandered in, crawling under the wooden gate. She didn't mind these, as long as a cow didn't barge in through the unlocked gate. That was when she roused herself to action, summoning every servant in the house, for the cow was a threat to the hibiscus tree.

She imagined each flower to be a waking eye, slowly opening to the light of day, slowly opening just a little bit more each day. She felt no sorrow when a flower wilted and dropped to the ground, for that was the way it was meant to be. Yellow, succulent flowers, flaring hugely in the warmth of summer and stubborn even in the midst of winter.

Janaki Devi, her mother, loved the hibiscus tree too. There was a simple explanation for her love. Every morning, whenever she cared to visit her daughter in Calcutta, the tree gave her flowers which she would then offer to the two images of her golden Lord Krishna and Radha, family heirlooms, in front of which she murmured her prayers each day. After her morning shower, Krishna's mother would softly walk down a flight of stairs to the front lawn, pluck a flower or two, and then return to the alcove where Krishna had ordered for her a low stool to sit on while praying and a low platform on which to place her beloved images.

Krishna remembered Radha and Krishna from her own childhood when they adorned a little room on the roof of her great-grandmother's home in Nabadwip, famous throughout the land as the birthplace of Sri Chaitanya, a mystical Hindu saint. It was not far from her father's village of Bishnupur, to which Janaki Devi moved after her marriage. To Krishna, Nabadwip, and Bishnupur through its proximity, were synonymous with Radha and Krishna, the imperishable lovers. In her mind, their carefree love suffused every human relationship, or at least was meant to, through some divine command.

Krishna had never known anyone from her mother's side of the family who was not a widow. So it seemed. They were amazing women, strong and proud even in poverty. Her grandmother, widowed at twenty three, lived alone with her great-grandmother. When she visited them as a child, during the summer, she would happily trudge two miles with her grandmother to bathe in the river each morning. Then they would rest awhile in the great Srirangam Temple on the banks of the river. They would sit in front of two large and hauntingly beautiful images of Radha and Krishna while many devotees sat on the stone floor around them and sang *kirtans*. The soft melodies of these hymns echoed in her ears all the time. She would sing or hum along too. Of course, if they happened to attend an evening service, the singing would be louder and lustier. But Krishna's voice remained soft and earnest at all times.

On the way back with her grandmother - sometimes Janaki Devi, her mother, joined them as well. They would stop to buy sweets and mangoes while her mother ducked into a bookstore to browse through or buy a novel. Back home, the fruits would be washed, sliced and offered, with the sweets and any other food her great-grandmother might have prepared in the meantime, to Krishna and Radha. It would be another half hour or so before the food was properly blessed and ready to eat. It tasted divine.

In Krishna's home, when Janaki Devi walked up to the alcove with her hibiscus she would also carry in one hand a small silver platter with grapes and sliced bananas, or apples or pears, and mangoes in the summer. If Krishna was home, she would sometimes sit cross-legged behind her mother while she prayed. Radha and Krishna looked the same as she remembered them as a six-year old. There were fruits laid out at their feet, somewhat meagre compared to her great-grandmother's days when there were always many more platters and different kinds of food. Of course, her mother's hibiscus, sometimes a solitary one, almost always lay grandly at Radha and Krishna's feet.

Some mornings, the hibiscus flower was larger than the two statues put together. The luscious yellow petals ribbed with bright red streaks trapped the two gods in a sea of color and passion. Krishna, dreamy-eyed, held a small silver flute in his hands while Radha's beautifully sculptured eyes seemed to be gazing at her mother, at Krishna, and just about anyone else who professed to be a lover of Krishna's.

Beyond the two images Krishna could see a silent pond with some slum-dwellers' huts sprawled at the edge of a line of palm trees. While she prayed or simply gazed at the statues, she would often find herself seized with an inexplicable longing for the dark, dank, almost tropical jungle that surrounded her grandmother's home where the hibiscus grew wild. Towering jackfruit and mango trees also stood on the modest grounds where monkeys romped and made faces at her. Snakes slithered in and out of a ruined, abandoned house that lay directly in front. And the overpowering smell of jasmine and *champa* flowers all day long, and all night long, cast a dreamy spell as they slept on mats spread on the roof under a starlit sky. In the only room next to where they slept, slept Krishna and Radha too - shorn of their finery and ornaments and crowns for the night. Their nearness drove all fear from Krishna's heart.

Krishna was not sure if her grandmother would have approved of her beloved gods being uprooted from the holy city of Nabadwip and moved to Calcutta. It was Krishna who dearly wanted to have the statues, and Janaki Devi was pleased and happy about it.

Krishna was sure her beloved grandmother would love

her hibiscus tree, and she persuaded Vikram to invite her and insist she come and live with her grand daughter, rather than her daughter in the village of Bishnupur. It was her fruit trees and her flowers that she missed the most when she came to live in Calcutta with Krishna, at Krishna's insistence, after her mother's death. She was happy to be staying with Krishna, and with Krishna's mother when she chose to travel from Bishnupur to join them from time to time, but she never forgave Krishna for having sold her house in Nabadwip. Krishna was young then, and was really trying to do what she thought would be best for her grandmother. If she were wiser, she thought she would've kept the place, even though it had none of basic necessities of civilized living. There was no electricity, no running water, and it filled her with terror as a child every time she went to the outhouse at night with the pale light from a lantern her only protection against snakes and mysterious rustlings in the leaves.

Her grandmother passed away quietly one day when Janaki Devi happened to be visiting Krishna. She claimed she was ninety-eight, but they all suspected she was well over a hundred when she died. One morning she sat, as she was accustomed to, in an old colonial easy chair - one of the few pieces of furniture Krishna had salvaged from a frenetic re-furnishing phase at her in-laws' fashionable home. The grandmother asked Janaki Devi to warm some milk for her, her customary drink in the morning. When Janaki Devi returned with the bowl, she was gone. Without a word, without a sound, without goodbyes.

Whenever Krishna felt exasperated with her mother, she would remember her mother showing signs of occasional exasperation with her grandmother and this made her feel a little less guilty. She and Vikram felt especially bothered every time they saw a beautiful hibiscus blooming in the morning and return later in the day to find it gone. This began to happen more and more frequently as the tree grew older and seemed to bloom fewer flowers. Some days there were only one or two blossoms. If one shrivelled up or dropped to the ground later during the day, there wouldn't be a single flower by evening since the second one would be lying at Radha and Krishna's feet. Krishna would complain sometimes, especially if they were expecting guests in the evening. It annoyed her to think the guests would be deprived of the special pleasure of seeing a beautiful flower growing right outside the drawing room window. But Janaki Devi would simply shrug her shoulder and say that the flowers would only drop to the ground the next day. It was better that they found a place at the feet of God before that happened. Whenever her mother returned to her own place in Bishnupur, Krishna missed her mother and her quaint logic. She wished she didn't have to go.

As the years passed, Krishna and Vikram found themselves casually exploring one idea after another in trying to take care of her mother's - and God's, they supposed - special need for flowers. The gardener worked relentlessly to grow other flowers – petunias, hollyhocks, sweet peas, snapdragons, sunflowers and numerous varieties of marigolds. Janaki Devi seemed utterly disdainful of all these flowers. Like a magnet, the hibiscus tree attracted the full brunt of Krishna's mother's piety.

Then came a terrible time when Krishna's father, the kind and eccentric Sambhu Narain, simply vanished from their village home in Bishnupur. In the past, he had disappeared from time to time and returned after a few days. On this occasion, the days turned to weeks, and the weeks to months. His two sons – Rahul, a wanderer like his father, and Sanjit, a dashing Indian Air Force pilot – rushed home to be with their mother. But they simply couldn't stay beyond a whole month, and persuaded Janaki Devi to move to Krishna's house in Calcutta until there was some definite news about about Sambhu Narain.

Much against her will, Janaki Devi came to live with her daughter. She grew sick and came close to refusing food altogether. But the hibiscus tree somehow gave her the will to carry on. Still disdainful of every other flower in the garden, including a rose tree that was beginning to flower beautifully, she simply moved back and forth between the hibiscus tree and hours of endless prayers in front of her Krishna and Radha.

Janaki Devi grew sicker. A time came when she couldn't come down the stairs any more. Her heart wouldn't let her. She had suffered a couple of heart attacks and was now tethered to an oxygen machine practically all day long. But she could look down from the upstairs balcony and see the hibiscus tree resplendent outside the large glass window of the living room. If no one was around to bring her a hibiscus when she needed one she would silently sink into a surly mood which seemed to poison the air inside the house. Those days when Krishna or one of the servants was around, she would specifically ask for a hibiscus, a knowing smile on her lips. Nobody would dare refuse her.

Soon she became too weak to even sit down for her prayers at the alcove. Still, she would come there to have her meals brought up from downstairs. Vikram, always the dutiful son-in-law, helped move the Radha and Krishna statues to her bedroom so she could look at them if she were lying on a pillow in her bed.

Now she needed more and more help and Vikram arranged for nurses, day and night, to care of her. One of them was always ready to run down the stairs and get her a hibiscus any time she fancied one. Strangely enough, the solitary hibiscus tree seemed always to have a beautifully formed flower ready for Janaki Devi.

Everyone thought her end was near. Krishna and Vikram often reminisced about those anxious days with Janaki Devi at her prayers, seated in a chair in her bedroom. She would look at them and then her gaze would travel back to Radha and Krishna. Some days she felt a lot of pain, and the nurse and Krishna had to help her up from the chair to her bed, sometimes with her breakfast or meal untouched. Then one day an ambulance had to be called to take her to the emergency. When they brought her down from her bedroom and were raising her into the ambulance, she raised her head to look at the hibiscus tree. Sure enough, it was resplendent with many full-blown flowers. Halfway to the hospital, only a mile from their house, the ambulance ran out of gas. The distraught ambulance driver complained that the driver on the earlier shift must have siphoned off all the gas and sold it on the black market.

Saddened and bewildered with the state of affairs in Calcutta, Vikram, driving behind in his own car, offloaded Janaki Devi from the ambulance and took her to the hospital emergency himself. For weeks she lingered. Throughout the months of October and November, the house overflowed with flowers, thanks to Krishna's ceaseless prayers to the Radha and Krishna her mother was so devoted to. At times, when Vikram looked at his mother-in-law's picture, the tears in his eyes blurred the flowers and the sprigs crowding around the photograph. It made him feel he was standing in a tropical garden in the centre of his home. The hibiscus tree stood outside the same room. No longer in its prime in winter, there were days when it would still give life to four or five flowers at a time. Vikram and Krishna took comfort in the thought that Janaki Devi would have loved that.

Christmas was a week away. At night Vikram and Krishna sat in the alcove where her mother used to sit. Under a dark blue sky the throbbing lights of the city glittered like the scales of some serpent risen from the heart of the River Ganga. Christmas was near, but there was little joy in their hearts, unlike other Christmases when Calcutta celebrated with endless rounds of parties. It was disconcerting to find a house of sadness so full of flowers. Clusters of azaleas, purple asters, bright red cyclamen, and yellow begonias – flowers friends were sending over with wishes for Krishna's mother's recovery. But no one really believed there was any hope for Janaki Devi as she lay in a coma.

They had declined invitations to all parties and were preparing to go to bed on Christmas Eve when the phone rang. It was the Woodlands Nursing Home calling. Krishna's heart seemed to stop. She held her breath, waiting to hear someone say that her mother was gone. Instead, the office attendant sounded alarmed and agitated. "There is this towering *sadhu* who has just walked into the nursing home, brushing past the night *durwan*, and gone straight into Janaki Devi's room," he said. "He has ordered the night nurse to leave the room and is now standing by the bed, his hands clasped, muttering prayers and mantras."

"What?" asked Krishna, incredulous. She looked helplessly at Vikram, not knowing what to say.

Vikram grabbed the phone from her and heard the man

at the other end repeat the same words he had said to Krishna.

"I don't know what to tell you," said Vikram. "How can we be sure he won't harm the patient?"

"I don't know, but we'll try to keep an eye from outside the room. The night nurse and the matron are doing just that."

"Don't call the police or do anything drastic," said Vikram. "We're starting off right now and should be there in fifteen or twenty minutes."

They reached the nursing home soon enough and found the attendant waiting for them in the foyer. Before he could say a word, Krishna and Vikram were running towards the room. The attendant followed. As they entered the door and stood in the room, the attendant, panting for breath, said, "What I wanted to inform you is that the *sadhu* left Woodlands moments before you arrived."

"What?" Krishna and Vikram both asked at the same time. But they found no words beyond that as they caught sight of a large crimson hibiscus held between Janaki Devi's hands over her chest. Then Krishna saw her mother, her eyes wide open, smiling faintly, whispering softly, "Oh Krishna, you've come."

TWO

AT LAST it was time to go. Time to take the trip she had been waiting for, patiently, for months. Not that the trip had been uppermost in Krishna's mind. No, in fact there had been a gaping void, an emptiness in her heart, ever since her brother's untimely death, under mysterious circumstances, that cast a shadow on the most trivial of pleasures. Nothing mattered. But now a semblance of peace had slowly returned to their respective households, her own and that of her in-law's.

As was customary every time they went from Calcutta for trips, they had to have a meal and then leave from Vikram's parent's home. "It is not right to leave home on an empty stomach," her mother-in-law said. Krishna resigned herself to further delays for she knew that even a stomach half empty was out of the question. And it took a lot of time, many rituals, to fill stomachs in Lady Ranu's home.

With summer knocking at the door, it would have made sense to fly to Bagdogra and then take a taxi to the Chirribilli Planters' Guest House. But here was a rare opportunity for them to travel together. They hadn't done anything like it since the day Malini was born. It didn't take too much effort to convince his employer's head office that the arrangements Vikram was proposing were in the best interests of everyone concerned. The company had nothing to lose, and had in fact always encouraged senior executives to place a high priority on family concerns.

Krishna responded enthusiastically to the idea of driving all the way. Once up north, there were so many places they could visit that they hardly needed to make any plans. Bishnupur had seemed a real possibility, since the village wasn't too far from their final destination. Krishna wrote to her mother. There came a strange reply written by Chanchal - a house keeper of sorts in her mother's home - which she didn't share with Vikram for fear of upsetting him. Apparently, her mother Janaki Devi was entering a fresh period of fasting and mourning for her husband, who had again vanished from the village, and would prefer a visit some other time. Krishna's heart ached for her mother and her somewhat crazy father. But there were other places she longed to be, and something kept telling her her father would show up again.

Even without the need for much planning, the trip turned out to be quite an upheaval. There seemed no way of avoiding a major turmoil. They ended up carrying everything from umbrellas to onions to sewing needles. Lady Ranu was not one to brush aside the company chairman's enigmatic words. "Odd things are going on in Chirribilli," he told Vikram. "Be prepared for the worst."

They had scarcely passed the outskirts of the city when the full blast of summer began to work its way into the car. Soon, everyone was drooping listlessly and finding it very difficult to stay awake. The only way Vikram could keep his eyes open and on the road was by wiping his face with a wet towel every so often.

Hamid, the accompanying boy servant, was obliged to stay awake too. It was his job to wet the towels from time to time. He soon found himself so tired that even this simple chore began to seem impossible. Hamid hated summers. In the little village where he grew up, summer always made him uneasy. It prodded something evil in nature, brought to life things vengeful, angry and restless. Like an angry spirit awakened from the dead, the hot winds of summer rose from the plains and smashed into whatever lay along its path.

The previous year, Hamid's father Noor Mohammed also died of summer, as many hundreds do each summer in this land. They brought his blind father home at high noon, his bloodless tongue clenched between his teeth, hanging from one side of his twisted face. The brown earth lay caked in his beard and in his nostrils. The brown set off the few grains of dull white salts that clung to his lips where the last trickles of saliva had dried in the sun. The memory of his father and the nearness of summer brought tears to Hamid's eyes.

Hamid had almost forgotten where he was. He quickly turned away his face to look outside so as not to give himself away to anyone in the car. He knew he was a servant, knew also that servants might often get away with their arrogance or insolence. But what he craved was strength, hoping it would raise him above the weak, ineffectual state of a servant. In many unspoken ways, both Vikram and Krishna had encouraged him in this.

The bushes and the long tufts of grass by the edge of the road bobbed up and down — a dusty, long and shapeless mass of green. Further away, the mango trees clustered together, a darker green, a little more solid, a little more still. But the squat hills in the distance hardly moved at all. Hamid had spent most of his life on the plain until his father moved to Calcutta. He always found the hills strangely uninviting, almost as disturbing as summer. Perhaps it was because he was always passing them by, never stopping to look around, never wanting to rest or explore in their midst. Hamid did not know for sure, but he remembered his father telling him once, "One is either a child of the mountains or of the plains; the one is always a stranger to the ways of the other."

Hamid made sure his eyes were dry. His thoughts returned to his surroundings once more. It had been a long trip, and they still had a long way to go. He was amused to think of himself sitting in the back seat all this while. Like a boss, he thought, when the real boss was in fact the person driving the car. His eyes swept over his own body in an involuntary glance. It brought a smile to his face. Who would say he was a poor farmer's son? His trousers were well pressed. His shirt collar was not frayed. A cheap ball point pen stared out of his shirt pocket and a not so cheap Japanese watch, a gift from Krishna, adorned his wrist. His sneakers were clean. He hadn't done too badly for a young servant. There was much he wanted yet. He missed Rahul, Krishna's brother who showed a great fondness for the servant boy, even though he had known him for only a few days. He might have prospered even more if Rahul had been around. But Rahul lived in a world of his own.

A smile flickered on his lips and vanished. Just as he did not want his masters to see him shed tears, Hamid didn't want them to see him smiling to himself either. It would probably embarrass him more than it would annoy Vikram. Their worlds were separate, their relationship born strictly out of necessity. Hamid was still too young to clearly define the boundaries of his world. But experience had taught him how unsettling even his most inadvertent forays into the other could be. Familiarity was almost always mistaken for impertinence.

One day a few months ago, Vikram had looked into his rear vision mirror and actually seen Hamid puffing up his chest, grinning, and pretending to blow smoke rings out of the rear window. At the time, they were driving slowly and painfully, Vikram softly mouthing swear words and curses, through one of Calcutta's impossible streets. Pedestrians spilled over the sidewalks like milling ants, blind to everything but their own little worlds. Hamid was clearly showing off for their benefit. Many of those outside were far too preoccupied to notice him. Some recognized him as a servant and thought him deserving a slap on the face perhaps. Others laughed at this mimicry of the upper classes. Vikram noticed too. Not knowing how to respond, and inhibited by the presence of a third person in the car, he made a joke of the whole thing. But that had not prevented Hamid from feeling confused and ashamed. Although he had no choice in the matter, Hamid preferred to sit in the front since the day of that incident. He was less self-conscious there, less prone to innocent mischief. But he could sit there only when there were no other passengers in the car. On this trip, Krishna sat beside Vikram, and Malini lay curled up in one corner on the back seat, fast asleep.

Vikram broke the silence. "You awake back there, Hamid?"

Hamid knew that the note of authority in Vikram's voice meant nothing. It simply provided the customary and perfectly natural way for the master to communicate with his servant. "Things are fine back here, *huzur*," he replied. "Even the little lady is fast asleep."

How he loved the little lady. If he had his way he wouldn't let anyone except her parents so much as touch a hair on her head. But he was smart enough to realize he had to keep his distance from her. People didn't take too kindly to men servants forming an attachment towards little girls, girls from respectable families.

"Good," said Vikram, after a pause.

This casual exchange woke up Krishna. She had been dozing fitfully during stretches when the sun didn't fall on her face. She murmured something to Vikram. Hamid couldn't understand what she said. He often wondered why they spoke to one another in English when he or any of the other servants were around. How nice it would be, he thought, to separate oneself from others whenever one chose to do so. Not through silence, but with words. He knew some English words, but he really wanted to learn the language.

His masters were good to him. Still, he knew he would leave them someday. Go to school maybe, and learn to speak English. But who'd pay him wages while he went to school? And what about the money he sent his mother? And how would it all fit into his plans for becoming a truck driver? Hamid could never see his way beyond these questions. Simple questions he could handle. Should he go to the movies or send an extra five rupees to his mother for *Eid*? It was a festive occasion when she'd need more money than other times. Should he be a little more friendly with the maid who made no secret of her liking for him? These matters were easily taken care of. The larger questions proved more difficult. They involved bigger slices of life, bigger than what life was prepared to deliver into his grasp.

He would surely move out someday. He had been thinking about it for the past few weeks. The more he thought, the more he remembered, the pictures flashing back and forth between far flung corners of time, tightening the muscles in his back. He would return to Hazariganj, his sad little village. To be congratulated and envied by the villagers. And he would marry the prettiest girl in the village . . . Saira, always wearing a scarlet petticoat, used to be so lovely, and he would've married her for sure. . . . Had it not been for what happened six years ago, he could almost picture himself in the servant's quarters bordering Vikram's family home. Since no other servants lived on the premises, he and Saira could've had the whole place to themselves — two little rooms and plenty of land to grow tomatoes, eggplants, and coriander. But the dreams vanished long before he had a chance to put anything together – one night when the villagers from Bishnupur raided Hazariganj. They smashed his dreams.

Hamid felt grateful to Vikram and Krishna for the life they had offered him, a Muslim boy from the village. He often felt like telling Vikram what a wonderful person and good Hindu he thought him to be, and how wretched the Hindus from Bishnupur were. They said somebody had polluted the Bishnupur reservoir with the blood of a cow. It hardly mattered that the water in the reservoir looked the same as any other water, and that no slaughtered cow was ever found in the neighborhood. Hamid was prepared to forgive them for all this, but not for what they did to Saira.

He could never understand why they had to destroy her honor, a wisp of a twelve-year old girl at that. When he was home two years ago, she reminded him of an animal. The scarlet petticoat had shrunk to a discolored rag. Half naked, Saira stumbled around the wells and the large tank, fighting with the dogs for the food some villagers placed near her from time to time. Her father didn't care what happened to her any more. He called her *junglee*, a barbarian, and didn't mind so long as she came no closer to his hut than the barn. Since the father could claim no compensation for what happened to his daughter, and since any demands might provoke further outrages against his family, he had wiped away all thoughts of his daughter from his mind.

Saira was only a year younger than Hamid. Folks in the village speculated on the long life that lay ahead of her and hoped she would drown or find some other way of ending her life quickly. Her wild eyes still haunted Hamid. Something told him Saira would never leave the village. She will sit forever, he thought, by the dusty paths, humming to herself, darting away like a frightened hare at the sound of approaching footsteps, even his own. She would throw stones at the dogs all day, and return the next morning from her father's barn to live out another day like the one before. Strangely, Saira was gone the last time he visited the village. She had simply vanished. Since nobody was ever found in the nearby tanks and wells, people imagined she had probably been abducted by somebody for his own use. Perhaps she had fled to the hills. Nobody really cared.

Hamid wanted desperately to return home. He wondered if Vikram would agree to make the slight detour. After all, Hazariganj was only about thirty miles off the main highway along which they would be traveling. But there were problems he didn't know how to deal with. What would his masters do while he met his friends and relatives? Would they let him get away before an hour, two hours? Perhaps it was too much to ask of Vikram.

He decided to ask the question after all. It took him a long time to muster enough courage to do so. Very diffidently, almost shyly, he asked, "*Huzur*, my village is not far from the way. Do you think you could stop there for a few minutes so I could see my mother?"

Vikram was startled out of his reverie by the question. He did not answer right away. He had grown extremely fond of Hamid. As a good master, he tried not to turn down his rare requests. He knew Hamid's village was somewhere along the way, close to the state border, but he had no idea how close. Even assuming a stop wouldn't delay them too much, it was the suddenness of the request that both surprised and annoyed him. At the moment when his thoughts were interrupted, Vikram was thinking of the stop that had been arranged for the night, the only one. His servant's ancestral village was far from his mind. "Where exactly is it?" he finally asked.

Hamid could barely conceal his excitement. "We go by bus from Siliguri to Pokhra. Then it is not too far." He probably wanted to be a little more specific, but was interrupted by Vikram.

"In any case," he said, "we probably won't be there till tomorrow evening. We'll think about it tomorrow."

If he was a bit disappointed to find Vikram uncommitted, Hamid remained silent. His enthusiasm was fired once more when he heard Vikram say, "Remember now, only your mother. If we do stop, I hope it won't be aunts and uncles, nephews and nieces as well."

"No, no, certainly not. I promise you that, huzur."

"That was nice of you," murmured Krishna, turning to her husband, as she fought off her drowsiness. "Actually, his village is very close to Bishnupur."

"Good Lord," exclaimed Vikram. "Now I suppose you'll want to stop by at Bishnupur too."

He had been there only twice since his marriage. While

Vikram had nothing against the place as such, there was one thing he dreaded —the excessive, unending attention lavished upon him by almost every person in and around his in-law's house.

Krishna started to laugh. "You know I won't. I thought I told you earlier mother wanted us to come when it was a little cooler. You'll make her nervous fighting the heat." She had not told Vikram about the letter from Chanchal suggesting they defer any visit. She decided not to broach the subject even now.

As silence settled inside the car once more, a little voice called out from the back seat, "Can I sit next to you, Mama?" It was Malini.

Even before Krishna could answer her, Malini was clambering to go across to the front seat. Krishna turned round to reach out for her as Hamid gently lifted her over. Malini snuggled herself comfortably between her parents. Everyone returned to their own private worlds. The car sped along, trying to run away from what was truly a murderous summer day. It seemed incapable of shaking it off. Vikram wondered what crazy impulse had led him to bring the car on this trip. This was to be something of a vacation for the family, yes, but somewhere along the way he seemed to have overlooked more intelligent forms of travel.

The heat continued to get worse. Together, heat and silence made the air very oppressive. "Didn't the boy go to his village only a year ago?" asked Vikram.

"Yes," replied Krishna. "His next vacation will soon be due. I don't suppose a brief halt at the village will do us any harm.

There are wonderful cooks in his family. Maybe they'll cook us a meal."

"Chicken and *parathas* may be all very well," said Vikram, "but we'll turn the whole place upside down. The women will refuse to stir out of their huts. The children will gather together and stare at us. There won't be any young men around for sure. There are so few of them in the villages these days. The old folks will silently smoke their pipes, ask us if we're comfortable, and secretly wonder why we ever came. Finally, we'll eat our chicken and *parathas* and leave. Do you really want to go through that ordeal?"

"If the boy is to be disappointed," said Krishna, "I hope you'll make it easy for him. He was pretty close to his father before he came to work for us. He must miss him a lot."

Vikram glanced sideways at Hamid, now dozing in the back seat, quite unaware that he had been the subject of discussion. "He's a good fellow," he said. "He won't mind if we don't go."

It was a wild, wicked summer outside, that summer of nineteen seventy-one. Almost as bad as the last three summers. From dawn to dusk, the sun glowed like an evil eye, its venom bubbling over through a fiery haze, now yellow, now purple, now lilac. It was unbearable, regardless of the time of day. The dust was heavy on the trees. It lay everywhere. Piled into the furrows of the skin, it overflowed the ridges in long, angry streaks — quivering like a cobra's tongue on fair skin, muted and hardly noticeable on brown. It embedded itself on the tongue and sank between the teeth. When the teeth worked, a grating noise filled the base of the skull and mushroomed through the caverns of a catatonic mind.

The leaves curled up into dry, listless shapes, drooped, and gathered dust. Cucumbers, pumpkins, beans, and other wild creepers lay down their gnarled stems and yellowing tendrils on the ground and on the rotting, neglected bamboo lofts. The leaves were indistinguishable against the branches and the landscape blasted by the sun. From a distance, the withered plants seemed to be one with the dirty bamboos and the crumbling earth. All day long, the countryside echoed with the mournful sound of cows as they dragged themselves through the heat. They tugged at the dry clumps of grass, the few that remained, as avidly as the vultures that plucked out the entrails of those that lay down in the sun and died. The buffaloes were silent. Their lolling mouths scraped the earth with every step. Only the cows persisted to the bitter end. The cows and the crows. The crows fluttered around the wells, shattering the stillness with their rasping, angry cries. Greedy and stubborn, they waited for the women to come fill their battered buckets and spill a few careless drops on the cobblestones. They watched. But the wells were dry, and the women had stopped coming. The crows would soon understand.

It was a time of the year when people speak little, particularly in the countryside. It is as if the tongue crusts over with the swirling dust and becomes useless to speech. But then, there is very little to speak of. Very little, except the rain. Nobody dared touch the subject of rain. Full of mystery, so capricious, it was almost a forbidden word. People were superstitious. Nobody broached the subject because they were afraid to quicken the fear in the hearts of others, afraid to betray the fear they themselves felt.

The muddy ponds slowly shrink into cracks that snake their clayey softness as far as eyes can see. Brooding villagers fill their earthen pitchers and buckets in these, and stare at the jagged cracks that widen each day and grow a little longer, a little deeper.

It is the same every year, this time of the year. For weeks, months, the sky spits poison on the earth. The rains, when they come, do not know when the earth has had her fill. Men are torn between hope and despair, stretching both to the farthest limits of endurance. They had been promised canal systems which would make floods a thing of the past, make them more self-sufficient in the summer. Some of the canals came, but so did the floods. Promises, promises.

Every so often, politicians and their admirers descended in their midst, proclaiming plans for new roads, electricity, schools for children, gurgling water all year round, doctors and hospitals. Remember the sign of the twin bulls, they said, or maybe the plough and the wheel. Their symbols changed, but the words were always the same. Their speeches over with, they would climb into their jeeps and hurry along to the next village. Sometimes, the men merely shrugged as they watched them go. Sometimes, they hurled obscenities at the departing figures, and the women covered their faces and blushed.

Their hooded, unseeing eyes fill with hatred as the men heave buckets of water in the afternoon, or wait for gritty mouthfuls of food to go down. They brood constantly. Their women avoid their dark looks all day, and submit in fear and silence at night.

A group of peasants working the fields raised their curious eyes. They straightened their backs as they peered into a cloud of dust rising in the south. Sometimes there were cars. Mostly, they saw trucks, traveling north or returning south, speeding with canvas sheets stretched taut over their cargo of shoes, medicines, tires, cloth, or tea. This time it was a car, a little blue car. Some of the men thought of the vast sums of money it must've cost. Others thought of life in the city from where it came. Life seemed to be easier there. Maybe so, some thought, but many a son, many a husband, never returned. They knew of wives and mothers who watched and waited for the prized money order or the letter which the mailman always promised the next day. It must be city women, thought some. Women were evil out there. The car passes by. The heads come down one by one.

"These fields are no longer green," said Krishna. "They've spent themselves after the last harvest. Everything is brown, almost dirty. They grow darker every moment. Soon the shrubs in the distance will be swallowed by the darkness." She turned to her husband. "Isn't it lovely, Vikram?"

"Sorry, I wasn't listening."

"I'm sure you were, Malini," she asked, turning to her daughter.

"I can't understand you, Ma," she replied. Krishna threw

her arm around her. "Oooh! don't press so hard," she cried. "You're hurting me."

"You know I didn't mean to," said Krishna, releasing Malini from her embrace.

"I know. It's nice to be near you, Mama." Turning to her father, she said, "Do you mind putting up the windows, Baba. Please."

"You can't be feeling cold," he asked.

"No," replied Malini, "but I can hardly keep my eyes open with this breeze. Besides, then you can't smoke any more." Vikram threw out his cigarette and lifted up the glass a little. "Tell me more about the fields, Ma," continued Malini.

"I can't see very much now. There are some tall palm trees not so far away. Only a little bit of their tops stick out against the orange sky. The rest is all in darkness." Krishna paused, and then cried excitedly. "Look Vikram, there's a man coming down one of those trees."

Vikram looked out of the window. Hamid, startled and awake, also turned his head in the same direction. He first thought it was a holy spirit, a *pir*, coming down from the tree, but knew right away it wasn't so. "Do you know what that man is carrying on his back, Malini?" asked Vikram. "He has an earthen pot slung across his shoulder. Inside, there's the best fruit punch in the world. Right now, he looks like a giant caterpillar looping its way down a twig. Do you know what a caterpillar looks like, Malini?"

"No," she replied timidly. "What if he falls down?"

"I've never known of one falling down," he said. "They say they can fly through the air. There's magic in their fruit punch."

Vikram laughed, but Krishna told Malini her father was talking nonsense.

Suddenly, she cried out, "Baba, that horrible smell. You couldn't have put up the windows." Covering her mouth and nose with her hands, she asked, "What is it?"

"Some dead animal, I suppose," replied Vikram.

"What does it look like?" she asked, screwing up her little face.

"Pretty ghastly, I should think," replied her father.

Hamid had dozed off once again. He was not expected to join in the family conversation. The others fell silent too. The crickets began to sing. Malini kept her face covered with her hands. Her father frowned as he concentrated on the empty road.

"Would you like to go to sleep?" asked Krishna.

"Yes, Ma."

Krishna pulled her to herself and said reassuringly, "We'll soon be there." Malini moved over without a word.

The little car purred along the narrow highway, its headlights sweeping over the tall grass whose blades bent and touched the cracked, uneven asphalt in the breeze. A rabbit darted out of the grass. It stopped for an instant in the middle of the road and stared into the headlight with startled eyes. The eyes, wide open and apprehensive, glowed like a dark wine. Only for a moment. Then they were gone. Hundreds of insects trapped themselves in the two beams of light. Many hurtled against the windshield, smashed themselves and disintegrated into little blobs of fluid. Vague points of yellow light appeared in the darkness, flickered among the few trees lining the road, and disappeared. The heat had melted the tar. The tires squelched over its stickiness with an eerie rhythm.

Vikram asked Krishna to take a look at the road map. "Wonder how much longer we have?" he asked.

The light was weak. Krishna's anxious face peered into the map as she tried to find a specific turnoff that would lead them to an Inspection Bungalow. Shabby old places, these rest houses never tried to lure the weary traveler with signs of welcome. They demand to be discovered, and there's always an element of drama connected with the discovery. Especially at night, when the traveler approached these places with equal measures of hope and anxiety. Government officials always received priority. So, discovery did not always mean shelter. The place may be fully booked, or reserved for some imperious civil servant and his family who may never show up.

Vikram was lucky. As the car rattled over the pebbles strewn over the dirt road and skidded to a halt in front of the cottage, a shadowy figure holding a hurricane lantern stepped out of a door. A red turban covered the old man's head over white, bushy eyebrows. Slowly, he walked over to the car. Lifting the lantern to the level of his shoulders, he looked enquiringly at Vikram. The kindly eyes set deep in the wrinkled face erased the uncertainty in Vikram's mind.

"My name's Vikram Mukherjee. I'm coming from Calcutta."

"You're most welcome, *sahib*," said the man. "If you'll just wait a minute, I'll go and fix up your room." The man walked away with the lantern.

"I'll follow him," said Hamid, opening the rear door and

stepping out of the car. He walked briskly behind the old man and quickly caught up with him.

After sitting uncertainly in the darkness for a while, Vikram began to fumble through his pockets for his matches. Alerted by the sound of the matchsticks rattling in their box, Malini cried out indignantly, "You're not going to smoke those horrible cigarettes again."

"When did you wake up?" asked Krishna.

"It must've been an owl that woke me up," she said. "Didn't you hear it?" When Krishna did not answer, Malini turned her head towards Vikram and asked, "Baba, do you know how they can even see at night?"

"I don't know if I could explain it to you, Malini."

Malini took her father's word for it and lapsed into silence. When she spoke again, there was a note of certitude in her voice. "Well," she said, "they should be thankful." After contemplating the owl a little longer, however, she came up with some doubts. "I wonder why they hoot and not sing?" she asked, addressing the question to no one but herself.

The *chowkidar* had not yet returned. Neither had Hamid. Krishna was beginning to get impatient. "Better go and see what the two of them are doing," she said.

"Yes," said Vikram and stepped out of the car. He turned his face to the countless stars that lay strewn across the sky to the east and vied with swarms of glow worms. He stood there a long time and stretched himself luxuriously. His joints and muscles tingled with a delicious pain. He walked towards the cottage with lazy footsteps.

It was a rectangular, white washed room with two large

beds. Hamid had helped the man fix the beds and had now gone looking through the house for a place for himself. These bungalows usually left servants and attendants to fend for themselves. It helped if they could quickly befriend the caretaker.

The old man was in the room when Vikram walked in. The lantern cast long shadows against the wall. Two flies bumped and buzzed against the lantern glass, magnifying themselves into two dark smudges that looped and lurched and met and parted on the wall. "What's your name?" Vikram asked the old man.

"Sitaram."

"Well, Sitaram," he said, "please get us a tumbler of water for the night. I don't think we'll require anything else. Tell me, do you boil the drinking water around here?"

"The water is from a well, *sahib*. One of the few around here that hasn't gone dry. It's very sweet." There was a slight pause during which the old man flashed his betel stained teeth in a smile. "All you big city men are afraid of cholera, aren't you?"

"Aren't you afraid of cholera?" asked Vikram.

"The only disease that frightens us is the disease that ends in death. In these parts, names don't matter. We have no doctors. We fear every disease really. It keeps us off our fields. It breaks up families. Makes widows. Takes away sons from widows." The old man paused for breath. "But I'm wasting your time, *sahib*. The water is pure. I'll get you some. And I'll also take care of your servant."

Vikram puzzled over the departing figure. Serene and composed, the man seemed perfectly at home with the pittance he made as wages, his squalid rooms, poor relatives, and so little to hope for beyond the next day. There was something unreal about such obvious happiness under such unlikely circumstances. He found it disquieting meeting such a person late at night. He wondered if he shouldn't be on guard for something odd or unexpected. But Sitaram inspired no fear. It was almost as if he had taken upon himself the task of settling scores on behalf of others with a whimsical creator, blow for blow, joke for joke. Vikram wondered what shrinks up a man's needs, banishes ambition, then transforms him into what many would consider a sub-human but infinitely happy creature. But he quickly chided himself for thinking of the other as a sub-human. There was nothing aggressive about the man, no fight in him. But what was there to fight for? In the final analysis, as his boss was accustomed of saying, Vikram found him almost grotesque, like the grin on a maggot-ridden skull which has little to laugh about. He walked away in confusion. He felt very tired all of a sudden.

There were clouds moving swiftly overhead. The sky was darkening fast. From the verandah where he stood, the car was a vague outline squatting low on the ground. A light appeared inside the car, a pale light that fell unevenly on Krishna's face as she switched on the dashboard light. Her face looked ashen. It reminded Vikram of her wistful face in the hospital soon after Malini was born. She looked so tender and fragile as she turned her eyes from the baby to greet him.

Vikram remembered the look of tortured disbelief the following day when she was told the child could not, and would not, see. Perhaps some day, but not now, was the verdict. He remembered the pity, the helplessness and the anger as, day after day, she would simply stare at the child in her arms, her fingers moving continually like feathers over Malini's eyes. Soon there was no pity. Only a passion that struggled to crush a senseless mistake in the ecstasy of birth. It was a fierce passion. Soon it came to be shared by Malini as well.

Vikram's mother mourned for weeks. "Why must this happen to our family?" she wailed. For many months after the birth of her grand-daughter, she could be seen moving in a daze from room to room, crying whenever she had little else to do. There was nothing to suggest that anybody heard her or took much notice of her. The rambling house on Chowringhee was built to withstand greater calamities than just tears. It was solid and cavernous. No matter what the time of the year, it was always cold inside. The sparkling marble floors guaranteed this pleasure, especially in summer. Blood-red Bokhara carpets, gigantic chandeliers, shining mahogany furniture by C. *Lazarus*. There was even a room full of mirrors acquired in moments of bizarre fancy by Vikram's grandfather. The mirrors picked up the cold floors and slammed them against the skin. Even the carpets felt cold. Vikram remembered how everyone avoided the room. Everyone except children who reveled in the fears and phantasies that excited their mind. Servants who swept and polished the floors did so without once looking up. They even tended to dust the mirrors with their eyes fixed on the ground. Lady Ranu could well lose herself in this or any one of a dozen empty rooms. Nobody heard her, except her husband Sir Ajoy. He had little choice in the matter.

One day, exasperated and driven out of patience, he remarked to his wife, "You must remember, dear, that for generations the Mukherjees have bred countless children with all their faculties intact. By and large, they were cretins or rascals. Who knows, this may be a change for the better."

Sir Ajoy loved his grand-daughter, and knew his wife did too.

Her husband's words may or may not have made any sense to Lady Ranu. At least, she seemed to back off a little from trying to smother every one of her acquaintances with her misery. Once more, people resumed their regular visits to the house without fear or embarrassment. The hostility towards Krishna that filled her heart after Malini's birth lost its edge in time. She soon resigned herself to the fact that she was saddled with a blind grand-daughter, and that was that.

In the early days, her mother-in-law's unspoken censure often drove Krishna to despair. No less galling were questions from other relatives who asked if her family had any history of cleft palates or missing toes. Perhaps there was a history of inbreeding in the family, wondered some. Others merely stared at her and thought how she could conceive such a disaster for the family. It was, after all, quite a famous family. Despite Sir Ajoy's cruel remark about cretins and rascals, it was true the house had contributed two brilliant barristers and several highly successful businessmen to Bengali society. One barrister was poisoned by one of his numerous mistresses. The family maintains to this day that he was driven to melancholia after his beloved wife suffered a stroke that left her speechless and paralyzed from the waist down. Sorrow led to his death, not poison, they believed. Of the successful businessmen, one leapt to his death from the roof of a bank, his own, after it crashed in the fifties. Two others, equally famous, went to prison on charges of embezzlement. The city leaders, the people who really mattered, were content to discount these common human frailties. They continued to look up to the Mukherjees for their charm and wealth. Sir Ajoy, in particular, never looked back from the day he married Lady Ranu. People still recalled with feeling their grand wedding reception where the band of the Gurkha Regiment played all evening, where none other than the Viceroy himself had toasted the couple, insisting, somewhat crudely and insensitively many thought, that the band play 'Roast Beef of England' during dinner.

Hamid helped unload a few essential bags from the car. Soon they settled in for the night. Only Malini seemed ready to bounce back to life at that late hour. She expressed her disappointment at being tucked in within minutes of entering the cottage. The others were too exhausted to match her energy.

In bed, Krishna shuddered as she remembered the early years of her marriage. She crept closer to Vikram. Half asleep, he put an arm round her neck and kissed her hair, mumbling something to the effect that he was glad the bed wasn't too large.

The sky was now completely dark. Occasional flashes of lightning showed masses of black, bloated clouds. The wind swishing between clumps of bamboos picked up the distant, mournful baying of jackals prowling the fringes of villages and cremation grounds. From nearby came the muffled flutter from the wings of bats and owls as they sliced through the night. The padded patter of mice scampering across the stained canvas stretched under the ceiling sounded like quick, heavy raindrops on the asbestos roof. Krishna rose to shut the windows. But there was no rain. To convince herself it was not raining yet, she stuck her arm out of the window and held it there a long time.

Afterwards, she walked over to Malini's bed. Although she had not heard her stir, Krishna wanted to be sure she was asleep. Carefully, she lifted an edge of the mosquito net and peered inside. She could not make out Malini's face. But there was another flash of lightning, and this time Krishna saw her. Malini's eyes were wide open, expressionless. "Why aren't you sleeping, Malini?" she asked.

"I'm frightened, Ma," she whispered. "I want to sleep with you."

It had started to rain at last. Krishna shut the window and slipped under the sheet. Malini immediately wriggled herself into her arms. The raindrops drummed all over the bungalow. It sounded like the wild, accelerated ticking of a thousand clocks. Only the fitful thunder broke through the monotony of the rain.

Three

SITARAM woke up while it was still dark. It was a little darker than on other mornings. He unfastened the chain on his door and stepped out of the room. The chain fell against the splintered door and clattered as long as it dangled in the air.

"Ramu, Ramu, get up," he called out to his son. His voice was shrill and trembling as he continued shouting. "Look, it's raining. Ramu, get up. Get up."

Eyes heavy with sleep, Ramu pushed himself up from his cot. When he fully realized what was happening, he sprang up with delight and came and stood beside his father. The sky was getting lighter in the east. Father and son gazed silently at the marvel unfolding in front of them. The drizzle sprayed their bodies and their clothes.

People had already started to move about in the surrounding fields. Men called out to each other. The listlessness of the last few months was gone from their voices. They walked with short, measured steps which pressed down on the soft earth and brought the mud squirting up between their toes. The earth had swollen and repaired the dry cracks, pores through which the rain trickled into its twisted guts. The ponds were already full. Little children jabbed and prodded buffaloes to the small depressions in the land that were now vast saucers of muddy water. This water soon turned to a sticky paste. For days, the mud remained caked on the animals. To dry, harden, crack, and finally peel off. Women converged on the ponds for water. They were greedy for water. Water for cooking, water for washing, water just for the hell of it. Many walked recklessly down the weathered and blackened steps into the water, stumbling over the loose and ancient stones, thrilling to the moisture seeping through the skin. They laughed and talked gaily in their dripping *saris* and walked home with heavy buckets and pitchers. Wet *saris* clung to warm bodies swaying with happiness, their wrinkles smoothed out over the skin to show an unabashed expanse of the hips or the tremulous softness of a careless breast, both delicately visible through the sari's transparency.

They left the inspection bungalow early. When Vikram held out a five-rupee note for him, Sitaram joined his hands in protest. "You were my guest, *sahib*," he said. "I'll be happier if you and your family remember us on your way back to Calcutta. We have rain today. What more can we want?" Reluctantly, Vikram put the money back in his wallet.

The dust had disappeared. The little huts looked as though they had been scrubbed clean during the night. The black tar shone on the road. They drove for miles and could not shake off the flat, oozing landscape. Nor could they escape noticing the slabs of stone, so easy to mistake for headstones to buried graves. Except that the names on the stones were names of towns, and the numbers gave distance, not dates. The rain followed them too. When they finally left it behind, they found themselves in mango country. The road wound through hundreds of mango trees. Under some, there were clusters of men busy gathering the fruits blown down by the storm. The fields and trees looked more lush and green the further they traveled north.

"Well, what will it be?" asked Vikram. "Siliguri or Darjeeling?"

Malini began clapping her hands delightedly. "Let's go to the mountains," she cried. "Let's go to the mountains. I want you to take me to Tiger Hill."

Vikram turned to look at Krishna. "Well?" he asked again.

"I thought you knew the answer."

Vikram was pleased. They had many hours of sunlight ahead of them, and the rain had made driving much more pleasant. Besides, there wasn't a decent hotel in Siliguri and it was never in his mind to stop there. It seemed logical to go to Darjeeling even though it was a little out of the way. He just wanted to hear Krishna say she wanted to go. Hamid too was pleased and excited by the prospect. For the moment, he forgot his earlier misgivings about mountains.

They had come to Darjeeling nearly six years ago. It was

a typical Bengali honeymoon in which the need to return to Calcutta haunts the pursuit of pleasure and casts a shadow on every smile, every rapture. Vikram had four days to spare. During the first two days, they walked for miles. They walked after breakfast, after lunch, before dinner and after. They walked what then seemed to be the entire length of the Himalayan range to see the races. Their feet were blistered after the interminable trudge from the hotel. Krishna wanted to cry, her feet hurt so much. Instead, they choked themselves laughing as the jockeys kicked each other, obstructed other horses, held back their mounts, and threw all the rules of the book smack in the faces of the solemn stewards. They wondered if the dour stewards could be laughing behind their inscrutable faces. The crowd loved it. While this foolery went on, they roared with laughter. Afterwards, they happily went home poor. The highest, and crookedest, race course in the world.

Then the weather took a turn for the worse. There was little to do but stay in the hotel. They grew restless and disappointed. In the evening, for want of anything better to do, they wandered into a photographer's studio. Last year, a friend told Krishna that their photograph could still be recognized on a dusty shelf in that struggling studio, forever ready to go out of business..

Vikram liked to tell his friends that the primary purpose of a Hindu wedding was to convince oneself one lacked the nerve to go through with it a second time. It took him three days, out of a total leave of seven, to get married. In the process, his knees became stiff and his tailbone throbbed painfully for days afterwards from sitting hour after hour on wooden *piris*. His eyes were bloodshot from the smoke and fire. Later, he was to claim an intense dislike for fire, which made him a reluctant participant in the festival of Diwali. Fire, the everlasting witness to their union remained for him a cause for much aggravation.

Like a dutiful Hindu son, he suffered in silence the endless debates, assessments and exhumations of family history. Well before the aspiring, or prodded, brides were ready for the final judgment, their ancestors and relatives had been chopped and ground like curry *masala*. Those who still retained any flavor and pungency, and considerable unencumbered property, only such families and their daughters warranted further consideration. Finally, as if impelled by pity to take him into confidence, Vikram's mother thrust before his eyes three photographs. These were the finalists. Vikram knew where his duty lay. He refrained from making any comments, which was exactly the way his mother wanted it to be.

There was little to choose between the three anyway. All three pictures were of attractive young women looking extremely stiff and ill at ease. But for the size of the pictures, and the fact that all three had been expertly touched up to reveal perfect features and flawless complexions, Vikram could well have been looking at police mug shots. Although curious to know whom he was getting married to, Vikram chose not to ask any questions.

Then they sprang a surprise meeting on him. Everything had been planned without his knowledge. All Vikram knew was that they were to go to Firpo's for dinner. Relatives were invited, as were a few close friends of the family. Shy by nature, Vikram retreated still further within himself in the company of uncles, aunts and cousins. He was propelled by an aunt past many an empty chair and eventually pushed into a particular seat out of reasons best known to the propellant aunt. Later, several minutes later, he realized he was sitting next to a beautiful woman looking down nervously into her lap where she kept twisting and unraveling around her fingers a corner of her dazzling sari. Vikram stared at her for a moment until he remembered her from the photographs. Normal conversation around the table ground to a halt, the mulligatawny soups remained unstirred, and Vikram felt every pair of eyes bearing down in his direction. His ears turned hot and scarlet. It felt like sitting in an examination hall, flunking all the answers.

If anything, they behaved as perfect strangers on their wedding night. Long after the guests had gone and the *shehnai* silenced its wail, Krishna sat expressionless in one corner of the bed, weighed down under a ton of golden brocade, gold necklaces, gold bangles, and gold bracelets. Her slender neck lay bruised under the sapphires and diamonds of ancient heirlooms. Her body was unaccustomed to the masses of gold and filigree, and she feared she would break out in a rash any moment. The women, dozens of them, took hours to dress her. She lost count of the times they loosened her *sari*, pulled it in, pulled it out, or gave a new fold along the drape. At one point, the sapphire necklace didn't look quite right. How could it, someone pointed out, sitting so high on the adam's apple. Don't choke the poor girl, someone said. No, thought Krishna, it's enough that you're asphyxiating me with hair spray. The mascara was a mess. Off with the lipstick, wrong shade. When all that was finally over, Krishna wondered what the rest of the night held in store for her. Later, she told Vikram how angry and frightened she was as she remembered the winks, the whispers and the giggles that followed her exit to the bridal suite.

She kept looking into her lap with the same expression as when he had first seen her. Vikram wanted to speak to her desperately. But he hesitated. After a while, he gave up the idea and went into the bathroom. He didn't shut the door. Instead, he went to a corner hidden from Krishna's view and changed for the night. When he finished, he walked up to where she sat and asked, "Won't you go to sleep? You must be more tired than I am." In retrospect, Vikram decided he could've phrased the question much more elegantly.

Krishna stood up silently and walked to the dressing table. She did not look at him. Slowly and methodically, she undid the clasps of her necklaces and laid them out one by one on the table. Vikram watched fascinated. She got down to the bracelets, and finally the bangles. She left six bangles on each arm and removed everything else. Then she looked at herself in the mirror and saw Vikram watching her with amusement.

That almost seemed a signal for her to pick up her nightdress and storm into the bathroom. Vikram was still watching when the door slammed shut in his face. He heard a click as the latch was pushed forward. At first he was puzzled, then he started to laugh, uncontrollably, and found it difficult to stop. When she came out, the makeup had been washed clean. She looked very pale as she walked into the light in her silken robe and proceeded to sit at the same spot she had occupied five minutes ago. Later, she put the blame for her churlish mood upon the robe's sash which she could not find. At that moment however she resumed staring into the darkness beyond the open window.

Vikram sat down beside her and lifted her hand in his. There was not a look or word from her yet. She even let him play with her rings. Quite instinctively, and without any visions of more tender overtures, Vikram put his hand on her shoulders. The abruptness with which she sprang up from the bed seemed to him grossly exaggerated and unnecessary, more so because of the gentleness of his touch. Suddenly, he felt the throbbing pain return to his tailbone. Vikram realized that his infinite patience was wearing thin. He made no attempt to follow her to the chair by the window. He simply switched off the lights and lay down. Taking it for granted she would follow him later, he was soon fast asleep.

He woke up with a start a couple of hours later. It took him a minute to adjust his eyes to the darkness. Then he saw her exactly where he had left her before dropping off to sleep. It bothered him even more because he had not intended to fall asleep. Vikram swung himself noiselessly out of the bed. Then, creeping up to the chair in which she sat, he bent down and kissed her softly. Krishna was startled out of her thoughts. All she said was, "Oh! it's you." The words sounded more a reassurance to herself than an acknowledgement of his presence.

Vikram kissed her again and knew she had been crying. He never knew what got into him then. Perhaps he thought of acting out some of the scenes familiar from cheap paperbacks and Hollywood movies. With a certain masculine firmness, he raised her from the chair and drew her close to him. He soon regretted having even thought of such things. Krishna flew out of his embrace and after a few undecided steps moved away to another window. Once there, she curled up her legs and sat down on the ledge.

As he groped his way back to bed, Vikram wasn't sure whether it was in shame or anger. Whatever it was, it almost made him blind. He crashed into the side of the bed and thought he had cracked his shin. He began to wonder if she was repelled by him physically, as one might expect her to be by a stranger. Surely, that was not the case. Was there an earlier love that made her so indignant? But he was just as powerless as she to fight custom and tradition. He too had found the idea of an arranged marriage outrageous at first. But what was one to do about it? Did she imagine he had trapped her for nights of pleasure, for a lifetime of erotic gratification? No, he was beginning to believe she must have another man in her life. As the night wore on, and he worked himself into a rage, this suspicion changed from a doubt to a near certainty.

Morning came with a knock on the door. Vikram answered it from his bed. It was time to get ready for the morning flight to Bagdogra. Once more, in total silence and complete privacy, they washed, brushed their teeth, and changed. Vikram found himself locked out of the bathroom until Krishna had finished. As a result, they were late getting away. All the while, Lady Ranu paced the corridor to soothe her nerves. Since the exercise didn't seem to be working, she took to knocking on the door every two minutes.

Of those who saw them off at the airport, quite a few were openly curious to read in their looks the intensity of the ravages of the bridal night. They drew their own conclusions, whatever they were. Sir Ajoy patted them reassuringly on their backs and sent them on their way.

On the plane, it struck Vikram that Krishna had spoken to him only once from the time they entered the bedroom after the wedding. He looked at her questioningly and forgot all the pain, the shame, and the anger of the previous night. Krishna was peeping through the drawn curtains into the hollow sky locked out of the aircraft. Vikram reached out and pulled the curtain. Pure gold of the morning sun rushed in through the oval window. Krishna blinked and ducked her head in surprise. Then she turned and smiled unexpectedly at him. A smile full of innocence, totally devoid of guile. As he drew his hand back from the window, Vikram touched her cheek lightly with his fingers. Krishna blushed. At that moment, that ineluctable moment in eternity, Vikram tasted love. The arranged love of arranged marriages, as he liked to call it.

As Vikram looked at Krishna now, he suddenly wanted to stop the car and kiss her. If Hamid hadn't been present, and he hadn't been climbing a steep incline, he might've done just that. Luckily, the crazy impulse spent itself by the time he hit a level stretch. They turned a corner overlooking a valley, and a gust of wind caught them unawares. Malini shivered in delight and flung her arms around Krishna. Vikram slowed down a little as Krishna slipped a cardigan down Malini's head and wrapped a shawl around herself. Even in summer, she seemed prepared for everything.

"Hope you don't catch a cold," said Vikram, turning his

head towards Hamid, making sure he was properly clad for the mountain air. The servant replied he was all right.

"Are there tigers on Tiger Hill, Baba?"

"Not that I know of, Malini."

"Then why do they call it Tiger Hill?"

"Maybe there were tigers there once upon a time. We must go and find out for ourselves, shouldn't we?"

"Yes, yes." Malini was thrilled by her father's response.

Soon they were in Darjeeling. As always, it was cool and beautiful. There were times of the year when one couldn't move ten paces in this resort town without recognizing a familiar face or drawing a warm hello. These were friendly times. They were also bad times, particularly for women who resented having their bottoms pinched in the Mall, or their shocked breasts tweaked in a flash by hawk-like fingers. Young men flocked to the town in droves. Apart from things they could buy at a resort—good food, wine, rosy-cheeked women — they tended to associate their romantic drives with the mountains. They came fortified in the belief that love waited just around the corner. Every swaying pony-tail hung baited with promise. Every girl at the bus stop seemed to cry out for affection. In the end of course one returned to the plains to sweat over fading visions of a young face, a pair of shapely legs, or the softness of unknown breasts and unidentified haunches. Strangely enough, they kept coming back each year. When the tourists left, the locals relaxed. Enlightened women pensioners smiled again as they went out on their regular walks, with their old walking sticks, their old dogs, and sometimes their old husbands if still alive and kicking, clad in their old tweeds. They breathed a little more freely, walked a little more briskly.

The season had almost come to an end now. There was plenty of room at the Everest Hotel. The carpets seemed frayed, the curtains faded, the attendants sullen. But Krishna was glad to get inside their room. The hotel clerks also promised to find Hamid a suitable place to sleep the night, at no extra cost. They had made good time on the road. There was still a little sunlight in Darjeeling. Malini walked confidently up Nehru Road, one hand in Vikram's. the other in Krishna's. They stopped at a soda fountain halfway to the Mall. They liked it here, out in the open. It was too beautiful outside to linger in the hotel even for a cup of tea.

"Let's go and sit on the terrace," suggested Krishna.

"What can we eat here, Ma? I'm hungry."

"You can have a milk shake or an ice cream."

"Can I have a strawberry ice cream, please?"

"You can have anything you want," Krishna whispered in her cars as she drew her closer to herself.

Malini smacked her lips contentedly as she licked the ice cream cone. She also loved the crackle of fresh wafers. So, before it could get soft and soggy, she broke off bits of the wafer. She smiled at the sound of her teeth crunching through the pieces. Vikram was busy scanning the Planter's Club across the street, hoping to catch sight of a familiar face.

"Look at those peaks, Vikram," cried Krishna. "Look, look, before the clouds cover them again."

Vikram turned his head to catch a flashing glimpse of a magnificent line of peaks taking their last curtain call before night set in, jagged little forms proudly lifting their head above a rushing torrent of clouds.

"Where is it, Ma?" cried Malini almost at the same time. In her eagerness, she tilted the remains of the cone, and down came the melting ice cream on her dress. But she was breathless with excitement, and quite unconcerned. "Tell me, Ma," she asked with even greater urgency, "Where are they?"

Krishna saw a minor crisis in the making and felt she had to intervene. "Wait a second, Malini," she said, taking away the half-finished cone gently from her hand and placing it on a plate. She moistened a corner of her *sari* in a glass of water which Vikram quickly held in front of her. Krishna gently wiped away the stains.

Malini thought she had perhaps done something wrong. She moved her face against Krishna's and asked in a voice which was barely audible, "Where are the mountains, Mama?"

Krishna gathered her into her arms. She was about to say, "There," when she stopped. The words froze in her mouth. The peaks were no longer visible. Only a solid wall of clouds stood against the sky. Malini spoke once more, "Can you see the snow, Ma?"

"Yes, it's beautiful. It's also very cold."

Malini suddenly remembered her ice cream. "Baba," she asked, "Does the snow look like strawberry ice cream?"

Although he had gone back to looking at the Planter's Club, Vikram heard the conversation behind him. He turned round to answer, but stopped as he saw the rising tears in Krishna's eyes.

It was Krishna who answered her question. "If they hadn't put the strawberries in the ice cream, it would've looked exactly like the snow."

Four

IN THE two days since Vikram and Krishna left Calcutta many disturbing events took place in North Bengal. The papers weren't writing about half of what was happening. Happy and unconcerned, they sat down in a secluded corner of the lounge that evening in Darjeeling. Not far from where they sat, a small fire burned steadily, the burning logs filling the room with the smell of pine and eucalyptus. Oblivious of the sputters and hisses that rose from the fireplace, Malini soon lost herself in the story of a brave and handsome prince. Her face showed wonder, excitement, and sadness as Krishna explained how the prince had fallen under the spell of an ugly witch who turned him into a frog and kept him a prisoner on the castle grounds. Malini was touched by the loneliness of the frog and the futility of his ceaseless croaking which no one took any notice of. She fell asleep even before Krishna had finished the story.

It was here that Krishna conceived Malini, in this very hotel. She had forgotten the room but remembered the view from the window quite distinctly — the same view of the mountains as on a clear day, but somewhere in the foreground, a little to the left, was a jacaranda tree and beneath it a grave. It was a small, white grave, nameless to her from a distance, strewn with leaves and dead flowers. The morning she left the hotel, she had looked out of the window and seen a bunch of red flowers lying at the foot of the cross. On previous days, especially when it rained, she had brooded over the forgotten coffin that lay inside. Now at last there was something to connect the lonely, moldering grave with the living. The flowers made Krishna so happy she cried.

Where could she have found so much happiness? She searched her mind for an answer. In two, three, four short days. And with a complete stranger? She questioned her motives, her instincts, to see if she could find some hint of dishonesty. She questioned her happiness and was amazed to find it so pervasive that it promised to transform every action, every thought. So when Vikram touched her shyly and hesitantly, so lightly as to suggest it was unintentional, she trembled. He felt the tremor, hung back, then pushed her robe away from her shoulders. The silk rustled like leaves blown by the breeze as it fell in a heap at her feet. He drew her to his naked body to find her shivering uncontrollably in the dark and thought she was afraid. She knew it was not so. He held her away from him so he could see her in the feeble street light that radiated through the blue haze outside the window. Her face was quite composed and peaceful. She read the care and passion in his face and held out her hands to him.

It was not any different five, six years later as she melted at his touch and lost her senses till she woke once again in a shimmering vortex. Before her enchanted eyes were silent mountains and golden poplars standing imperiously on the banks of ice-blue lakes sworn to perpetual stillness. The storm of their surging flesh linked them not only to each other, but to everyone else. She could never tire of the sensation, never feel sorry about the fleeting expectancy, the ebbing exuberance.

As Vikram drew away tonight from the maze of soft ripples and fragrant skin, he did so as wordlessly as always before. He straightened the blankets over Krishna and saw her face as quiet and peaceful as ever. He gave her a last kiss, full of gentle passion, of unspoken love, whispering only the silent gratitude of their union.

After breakfast, Vikram went down to check out the news from the gardens. "They've set fire to some huts in Goalpara and elsewhere in the Brahmaputra valley," said one of the receptionists. Otherwise, everything was all right. There seemed to be no trouble on the road, and the traffic no different from any other day. The absence of any further hint of trouble over the national radio news from Delhi only confirmed that the earlier assaults involving Bengali workers and government officials were probably no more than the local Assamese settling old scores. The newscaster quoted the Minister for Information as stressing the need for moderation on the part of newspapers in their day to day coverage, clearly a barbed reference to the perpetually emotional content of the news from Calcutta.

"Hold your peace," the Minister seemed to be warning, "or you may run out of imported stocks of paper."

Though the sun was bright that morning, the mist lay heavy on the nearby ridges. The pine trees looked wet and dirty. Silently, the porters loaded their luggage into the car under Hamid's watchful eyes. Krishna disappeared unnoticed to a place she remembered. She had spotted the old grave across the fence, but there were no flowers today. The mist gave the place an air of unimaginable sadness and foreboding.

She was back soon. As she walked to the car, she was caught in a stream of dew-washed sunlight suddenly breaking through the mist. Vikram stared at her in admiration, secure in the exclusive possession of that disarming smile, the beauty of the oval face, and the warmth of those arms, the more ravishing for their fullness.

Krishna pulled Malini close to her. Then, with unwavering patience, she kept talking to her, picturing for her a train that followed them, lost them, and found them again as it rounded a sharp corner and headed down for the plains. Vikram wasn't up to much when it came to keeping a conversation going with Malini. Still, he tried to be helpful and completed the picture by describing the young Nepali boy sitting on the fender of the locomotive engine and singing away as he scattered handfuls of sand on the tracks. He avoided having to translate the song for Malini's benefit by pleading ignorance of the Nepali language. Krishna found herself bogged down in complex theories of mechanics as she tried bravely to explain why the boy was throwing sand on the tracks. When she found Malini giggling over her mother's incomprehensible physics, Krishna thought it wiser to switch to descriptions of Buddhist prayer wheels and flags that loomed over the road at every corner. Her sweeping commentary didn't miss a single passing car or truck. The monastery at Ghoom, the Jesuit seminary at Kurseong, culverts, bridges, hairpin bends, and mooing cows all crowded into her pictures.

There was a brief intermission for Krishna when Vikram stopped the car to describe the glorious view from Coronation Bridge. When they started off again, Krishna had to describe the invisible foothills of the Himalayas and the raging river several hundred feet below. When she came to describe the concrete tigers sitting on the approaches to the bridge, Malini raised her hand to her wide open mouth in a gesture of shocked remembrance. "Baba," she said anxiously, "we forgot to find out about the tigers on Tiger Hill."

Vikram permitted a note of self-reproach to creep into his voice. "I'm sorry, Malini. That was naughty of me. I promise I'll take you there on our way back."

He looked at Krishna and asked if she wanted a break. It was Malini who saved her from losing her voice by asking if she might go to sleep in her lap. Even without waiting for an answer, she stretched out her feet over the seat and put her head on Krishna's lap. When she found her hand moving playfully through her hair, Malini drew it to her chest and covered it with both her hands. Krishna and Vikram marvelled in silence at this pantomime, this pure amorousness.

They passed lazy fields drooping with the harvest. The forest too was thicker here, bursting with pines, poplars, eucalyptus, ferns, and other trees that would always remain nameless to the untutored traveler. The ground was scorched in places where they had burned the choking foliage. Solid, blackened barks of trees stood as if to complain. Scrawny men with shining bodies swung heavy axes at the trunks, two to a tree, one on either side, swinging alternately, grunting with each blow.

They passed hordes of cows and the odd buffalo poking its eyes and moist snout through muddy ponds. Shriveled men with protruding bones prodded the freshly tilled lumps of earth reverently with their sticks. Bare buttocked children unashamedly relieved themselves by the roadside. Bare buttocked elders defecated in a similar fashion, but a little removed from the highway, their eyes averted from the road for the sake of modesty. Children walked to school, yelling to be heard over the sound of the engine and the air whistling by. There were children who waved their arms in delight and women who covered their heads at the sound of the approaching car. Other women straightened themselves from sweeping their courtyards, looked curiously at them, then returned to their chores.

They passed gardens. British tea gardens with Indian names oddly and mysteriously spelt. Women plucked tea leaves in some of the gardens bordering the highway. The baskets stood poised on their backs as their deft fingers found the leaves and buds with accustomed ease. They ignored the admiring glances they drew. Dark, proud faces, dark, firm arms, firm breasts thrusting out of the blouses, and neat round buttocks that had been the undoing of many a promising planter.

Occasionally, they saw a girl or a boy with skin several shades lighter than the others, a sure sign that an alien gene had slipped somewhere into their ancestry. At least they didn't see any blue-eyed, blonde kids like the *Santhal* children they once saw in the hills of Chotanagpur not far from the site of an explosives factory German engineers had helped to put up.

"One must admit," said Vikram, "that sex in the Dooars is not divorced from a keen sense of social responsibility. It's quite easy to find a home for the children of fallen British planters with the missionaries around here. Rarely will you hear of a child being abandoned."

"Surely, that was in a more sentimental time," said Krishna.

"You're right. The new generation of Indian managers would do well to keep up an honorable tradition."

Vikram had little respect for Indian planters who were, by and large, a scruffy lot, lacking class. The large commercial houses of the *Raj* always contributed generously to the cost of running the children's shelters, even those corporations who had no direct connection with the tea industry. The old chaps always stayed marvelously close to one another, lending a helping hand here, bucking up a disgruntled expatriate there. Nothing cut across their solidarity, certainly not Indians, no matter how often they tagged along with Englishmen on the cocktail rounds. Apart from cooks, *kanchas*, and *ayahs*, few local Indians ever came anywhere close to an Englishman's life.

Vikram imagined that religion might be the one thing that could cause a break in their solid front. He remembered once approaching his Chairman for a corporate donation to the Cheshire Homes for whom Krishna worked as a volunteer. Chairman Hammond-Barnett was adamant. "You'll never get me to contribute a cent to the Catholic Church," he said. Vikram tried to reason with him that the Catholic Church had nothing to do with the Cheshire Homes except that Leonard Cheshire, a great British airman of World War II, was a convert to Catholicism. "Don't you believe it," thundered Hammond-Barnett. "The Catholic Church is the greatest instrument of extortion ever seen in history. It's like General Motors. It doesn't need any money."

These and other thoughts kept them going through the day and into the afternoon. It was so much more pleasant than the day before. They rolled the car windows down and breathed in the moist mountain air. They stopped for a leisurely lunch along the way. Krishna chided Vikram for driving at less than his usual speeds. "Now we've missed the chicken and *parathas* in Hamid's village," she said, as she passed out the sandwiches.

Hamid didn't seem unhappy. "We can still fix you up a great meal if you care to stop long enough," he said. He realized they were running behind schedule, and still had another four hours or so before Chirribilli. "It's all right if you decide not to stop at Hazariganj," he added, always thoughtful, always accommodating.

"We'll see," said Vikram. Little did he know they had only a few hours before their rendezvous with fate.

They reached the provincial boundary between Bengal and Assam towards evening. An eerie stillness hung over the land. The Indian countryside is normally quite still. But this was different. This stillness was laced with fear. Even Malini began to whimper without any reason. She kept saying she was scared.

Nervous and uneasy, Vikram instinctively slowed down at first. Perhaps Malini was becoming car sick. He pulled up to the side of the road. As he did so, four heavily laden trucks swept past him in quick succession. Hamid, brisk and attentive, took advantage of the stop and poured out hot tea for everyone. There was milk for Malini in a smaller flask, but she didn't want any.

Vikram felt troubled over whether he should go on or turn back. He preferred to keep his anxieties to himself and would not ask Krishna her views. He knew the decision would have to be his. They were not too far from Hamid's ancestral village. But stopping there seemed out of the question at this time. Sensing his master's uncertain mood, Hamid did not broach the subject either, even though his heart ached to go home. There was a short ferry crossing ahead, and they might still make the ferry before it got too dark. Vikram decided to press ahead.

They had hardly seen a soul along the highway all evening. Everything was quiet and uneventful for the next half hour until they came across an unexpected roadblock. Vikram slowed down. It was a mistake. From a low-lying ditch by the side of the road, there suddenly came out a murderous mob, rending the sky with their howls, charging towards the little car like hungry animals.

Some of the trucks which had overtaken Vikram's car earlier in the evening didn't get very far either. As they worked their way in the direction they had come from, the trucks found an entire hillside on fire, a smoking, hissing inferno. Smoldering tree trunks stood upright on the slopes like pillars of molten steel. From time to time, branches crashed to the ground, shattering into a thousand sparks. Flaming tongues darted up in the crimson darkness as the ebbing fire licked the leaves and twigs scattered on the ground. The playful wind fanned the flames, and the fiery shades throbbed, deepened, faded, and deepened again.

Kirpal Singh, driving the truck in front, rolled up the windows in his cab as he skirted the fire along a narrow dirt track and left it behind. Once more, his sad eyes followed the sweeping beams of his headlight. The empty truck shook and rattled as it crashed through the darkness towards Siliguri, the bleak town at the foot of the mountains below Darjeeling. Three other trucks followed. All were empty.

They had been happy to dump their freight on the road and turn for home. These trucks meant a lot to them. For nearly five years after the country's independence, their families starved, scraped, and saved. They peddled fountain pens, moth balls, safety pins, needles, toys, and razor blades — just about anything to keep them going until the day one had enough to put down a deposit on a truck. The trucks meant far more to them than the cargo. They decided to let the looters do what they pleased with the medicines, the shoes, and the jute. Kirpal and the other truckers were happy to get away with their trucks and their lives. Had they been men from Bengal, instead of from the Punjab, they would never have gotten away so easily.

Kirpal Singh always thought of the lighted dashboard panel as a small radio. Tonight, it became a portable battery-operated radio in a city called Lahore many years ago. After their meals each afternoon, the women sat circling the radio. Sometimes they listened at night as well. They were good songs with old fashioned melodies expressing old fashioned sentiments. If the men in the next room complained that they couln't hear, as they frequently did, the women would turn up the volume for their benefit. The men laughed and sang and played cards. The most sought after cards being those with nudes splashed across their backs.

Kirpal Singh remembered the laughter as well as the terror. It was a dark night, darker still because the electricity had been shut off. There was confusion all around. Then flames began to shoot up from shops and homes, and smoke that choked and racked the lungs. And hideous screams. Even the voices over the radio were unreal. The killers came the next morning. As Kirpal sat hidden in a tree, he heard the shrieks. First his mother, then his sister. Even his grandma, well in her seventies, found no mercy. He heard his brother's terrified call for help, just once. He remembered his father moaning. And a chilling scream he did not recognize but which continued to haunt him for many years afterwards. His father called once more and then became silent. Somebody laughed, a heavy, mocking, reverberating laugh. Then the voices faded away and the laughter died down. Only the echoing screams remained.

In the smoke-filled darkness of the evening, he saw Harjit Singh pass beneath the tree. There was a gun in his hand.

Kirpal's throat was dry, fever shook his body. Harjit froze in his tracks as Kirpal's choking, rasping voice called out to him. As they walked up the street together to the last train out of Lahore, Harjit pressed Kirpal's face hard against his massive chest, his gnarled fingers covering the child's eyes. But in spite of the gathering darkness Kirpal had seen enough in the first few moments as they went slipping over slime that was blood, stumbling over objects that were once human. Children with bellies ripped open, young girls curled up in pools of blood. Bodies with faces of men but with nothing to show for their manhood, their manhood stuffed inside nearby bodies of women. The stench of hell hung over it all and tore at his gorge.

As the trucks roared through the deserted highway, Kirpal Singh kept muttering how he had seen it all before, so often in fact that the daily news others talked about seemed frivolous and absurd. He kept muttering how someone was always butchering someone else. "I'll be ready the next time," he muttered under his breath. "Ready and armed."

Kirpal stopped in the middle of his thoughts as the headlights picked up a fair, slender girl lurching slowly across the road. He braked violently and came to a stop only yards away from her. A thin streak of blood dribbled down her half open mouth. Her dress was ripped and smeared with blood. Trickles of blood ran down her legs and stained her torn, white feet. They cleaned her up with whatever water and rags the drivers and their helpers could find among themselves. Then they helped her into the last truck and let her lie in one corner of the cab. She huddled and shivered in a dirty sheet and did not utter a word. Just kept staring at the night with her swollen mouth half open.

Kirpal became more aware of the details around him, like small dark patches of burnt earth, perfectly square or rectangular, charred remnants of what might once have been a tea shop for truckers. The tire repair shop was also gone, remembered only by the thick curls of black smoke hanging over the site.

The trucks picked up speed again. They passed a thin, sickly man, all skin and bones. His wife walked beside him, carrying a small brass pot on her head and a baby on her hips. The couple looked up plaintively at the passing trucks. Kirpal slowed down a little as the old man weakly lifted an arm, asking the trucks to stop. But he felt uncertain about what might be lurking in the trees and shadows bordering the highway. With the other trucks almost upon him, Kirpal accelerated once more. The old man's hand came slowly down as the trucks thundered past.

Kirpal felt a certain kinship with the couple on the highway. He too had been resettled several times like he knew they would be. First on the streets, then to the railway platforms at Calcutta's other station, Sealdah, to join the thousands already there. That was the customary route. Perhaps the old man had been there once before, after his mud hut had been blown into the air like dust, all because two hundred miles away from his village, in the bustling Kidderpore area of Calcutta, a sacred *shiva linga* had been turned into a sausage by a rubber condom stretched around it from tip to base. It was taken for granted that a Muslim, obviously a Pakistani agent, had slipped the loathsome object over the stone phallus, and forty Muslims lost their lives in the riots that followed. People cracked each other's heads like ripe coconuts and set aside their meek and mild manners as they hacked away with knives at human flesh as far east as the province of Assam and west to Bihar.

The trucks approached a winding stretch of the road, slowed down, and passed another hut which had stopped burning halfway through. The smoldering logs lit up the stage for a twisted human form in the centre of the hut, caught with its legs arching out over one another, the feet straining to touch the earth, the arms twisted in a bow-like shape, crosswise, one hand pointing to the sky, the other stuck in an armpit more black and charred than the night. The teeth stood out, white, clenched teeth bared in a hideous smile.

Shortly after they passed the village, they came upon the blue Fiat burning in the ditch. Kirpal remembered having passed the car earlier in the evening. This time he decided to stop. As the trucks skidded to a halt one by one, a dozen men brandishing sticks and knives started to run through the fields. They carried with them stuff they had looted from the car and what appeared to be the lifeless body of a woman. Kirpal and the others climbed out of their trucks warily and walked back to the fire. They found a pair of dark glasses smashed by the side of the road, then a mud-stained shoe a few feet away. A little further still, in a clump of tall grass, they found Vikram, his half conscious body propped against an embankment, blood oozing from his nose and a deep gash on his temple.

Kirpal Singh tore a few strips out of his turban and bandaged Vikram's head. Many years later, he said it was a symbolic gesture destined to bind their lives together. The men pulled out some cushions and rubber seats from the trucks and spread them out on the back of Kirpal's truck. They laid Vikram down on these. With two of the helpers sitting alongside the inert body, Kirpal began to pull away. The others prepared to follow.

As the last truck was revving up its engine to move, the girl heard a faint moan. Stop, she cried out, gesturing frantically for the ignition to be turned off. They listened. This time everyone heard the sound. The driver leapt out of the cab and found Malini in the grass not far from where Vikram had fallen.

Kirpal and his comrades didn't stop their trucks until they reached Siliguri. They headed straight for the general hospital, where the doctors and nurses in the emergency ward worked late into the morning to save Vikram. The hospital had never seen a white woman, especially one walking in with a colored child in her arms. White women never came to the general hospital. Their husbands or parents from the tea gardens always took them to Calcutta or London for any medical attention. The doctors and nurses were curious about her, but a certain diffidence got in their way that night. Next morning, one of the visiting doctors blurted out, "You're so pretty, why did you marry an Indian?"

The woman explained that she was an American traveling through the province, and that the child probably belonged to the still incoherent man. Her name was Alice Newton.

Vikram finally regained consciousness, but remained in a

state of shock for many hours afterwards. His head swathed in bandages, he shuffled around the ward painfully, aimlessly. He stared foolishly at Malini lying in Alice's bed. "That's not her mother, that's not my wife," he muttered repeatedly as he moved from bed to bed, staring at other faces, hoping to find Krishna in their midst. He didn't know who to ask about his wife. There shone a glimmer of understanding in his eyes when one of the nurses pointed out that Alice too had been brought in by the truckers. But the light soon vanished and he asked, "Where's my wife? I must find her."

Alice concluded that hospitals mirrored hell, the hell that lay outside and almost sucked her in the night before. She was surrounded by peasants and laborers, past caring about the little decencies that separate the polite from the boorish, and impervious to curiosity. All morning, she watched one of them tossing his head from side to side, his eyes bulging with pain, gasping for breath, hurling his head up from the pillow to tear at a mouthful of air. The nurses came and went. Another whimpered continually, his pillow dark and wet with a green ooze trickling from his mouth. Sometimes the sounds rose above the crisp footsteps of the nurses and the noise of instruments, bottles and bowls. And Alice wanted to run.

The little girl was not her problem. One of the nurses said there was something very wrong with her eyes, but that was not Alice's problem either. She wanted to be with her own people, so she could forget all the foolishness, all the madness. For the moment, the safe haven of the British tea garden at Chirribilli was all she wanted. That was where she was headed for in the first place.

Some of the doctors arranged for one of the hospital Jeeps to take Alice to the garden. The little girl whimpered a lot, reached out for Alice a lot. But if she felt anything for her, Alice brushed it aside as the Jeep rolled past the lush forests and wet fields with the occasional Himalayan peak flashing between the trees.

Half an hour later, Alice Newton changed her mind. She wanted the Jeep to turn back and return to the hospital. Once there, she wanted to go straight for Malini, to lift her in her arms, and cling to one another.

But her words remained locked in her heart, for it seemed a foolish thought. How could she ever imagine herself a mother to Malini, a replacement for the mother she had lost. By the time the Jeep arrived in Chirribilli Roger Ames was nowhere to be found. And the servants were tightlipped.

Five

RETURNING FROM his customary game of tennis in the evening, Roger Ames was unhappy. What in blazes was he doing there, he asked himself, as he washed down some onion fries with his gin and bitters. The evening was silent and sticky, the servants worked noiselessly through the house, and the spirits of planters buried in flower-laden English graveyards came back to visit him, as they did every evening around this time. The *Raj* had come and gone, but nothing had changed for the servants. As manager of the Chirribilli Tea Estates, Roger knew that history and decay were fast overtaking the expatriate Englishman in India. He knew his days in the tea gardens were numbered.

Roger gulped down a large mouthful of his drink and felt the tangy sweetness spread its warmth through his body. He stretched himself luxuriously in the cane-backed easy chair dominating the verandah and lifted his legs over its seemingly endless arms. The tension still throbbing in his limbs from the sets played a half hour ago clashed oddly with the quiet settling down around him. "Kancha," he called out in his deep voice, and a short, fat man in white shirt and white trousers suddenly materialized in front of him.

"By George," he exclaimed, "you're already moving faster than you've done in months. Could it be you're beginning to lose weight?"

Kancha smiled meekly as he knelt down to untie Roger's tennis shoes. He didn't answer.

It was exactly two weeks ago that Clarence Ames, Roger's father, left for Tunbridge Wells. Already, Kancha was showing signs of returning to his old self. The last two months of Clarence Ames's visit to his son's bungalow had devastated the servants' sense of discipline. The old man had dropped by for what he said would be a couple of weeks rest during a journey from Sydney to London. But the two weeks had stretched themselves to four, six, eight weeks, and still Clarence Ames showed no signs of moving along. "My son," he said, "this is the peace I've been looking for all my life. I've searched for it in the great Australian outback, on the prairies of Saskatchewan. But nothing, absolutely nothing, can compare with the mystical harmony that has taken hold of me here in Chirribilli."

Several weeks passed before Roger realized that the peace his father coveted most was the peace of the late afternoon when the bungalow was almost deserted and Roger himself was in the factory. This was the sacred hour when Clarence Ames sat down to enjoy his afternoon tea served meticulously by Kancha. It was a ritual which Kancha, on account of his undisputed seniority among the servants, soon began to actively participate in each day.

One afternoon, when Roger unexpectedly returned home to collect some papers he had forgotten, he was amazed to find his father and Kancha seated majestically on the rear verandah, staring blankly at each other over Roger's finest silver tea service. "Simply trying to break down some preposterous class barriers, my boy," announced Clarence Ames in his usual bluff manner.

"Why didn't you call the other servants too, father?" asked Roger sarcastically.

"Ah!" answered his father, smiling benignly, "but this is only a beginning."

Kancha vanished inside the house as soon as he saw Roger. Now Roger lifted the cover of the teapot to see if there was anything left. Why not break the ice, he thought, by joining the old man over a cup of tea. He was totally unprepared for the whiff of whiskey which rose to his nostrils.

As he saw his son staring into the depths of the teapot, Clarence Ames was quick to exclaim, "What have we here, another miracle in the middle of the tropical afternoon? Hah! Clarence Ames changes Darjeeling tea to Johnny Walker Black Label." As his eyes met his son's, he added, "Now you know why I didn't call the other servants, eh? That would be squandering your wealth, like casting pearls before swine."

Roger Ames was a confirmed bachelor. His entire household consisted of his retinue of ten servants. He hated unpleasantness, and did not wish to appear heartless in front of his servants. So he allowed his father to stay on, allowed Kancha to remain in a drunken stupor each night, and felt gratified by the knowledge that his father would probably leave once the last drop of scotch was gone, and that his rapidly diminishing stock of spirits could always be replenished at the company's expense after Clarence Thomas had left. Eventually, that's the way it happened.

Kancha gently pushed Roger's feet into a pair of slippers and walked away with the tennis shoes. Roger remembered that the fresh stocks of liquor and wine had arrived earlier in the day. So had a memo from the company's Calcutta head office highly critical of the mounting expenses and declining production at the Chirribilli Estates. As an added insult, they were even sending down an Indian executive to audit the accounts and file a special report.

Roger had been in India for only five years. He had no first hand knowledge of what things were like in the pre-independence days. But he was certain it would then have been impossible for an Indian to investigate an Englishman. Since he was not one to hide facts, Roger couldn't care less what the Indian manager found. He felt quite resigned about the possible outcome. In any case, he was beginning to tire as much of the bureaucracy as of the political activists creating trouble among his workers.

From deep within the bungalow came the sound of running water. Roger found it getting faint and distant as he turned his attention to the pinpoints of light erupting unexpectedly in the dark. A sturdy wire fence stood between those lights and the manager's bungalow. It was intended to keep out snakes and wild beasts. Some nights when the spirits were about, Roger would look down upon himself from their midst and find the glow from the tip of his cigarette almost indistinguishable from the lights in the distance. The moment the spirits left, he knew there was a difference. Those lights were as far away from him as England. He could go back to his home in Tunbridge Wells, but the distant huts would forever be barred to him.

When he first came to this country, Roger had seriously hoped to bridge some ancient differences, to treat servants as human beings, and Indians as friends. It took him only a few months to realize that reticence was still the Englishman's most potent strength, and that true friends could only be found among one's own kind. The Indians who came close to him socially or professionally were inclined, as a rule, to squeeze whatever profit they could out of the friendship. As for those on the lower rungs of the ladder, it seemed they had no idea how to respond to anything other than abuse, however benign, which had become almost second nature to them.

There were other fences that crisscrossed through their lives, like the one separating those who grew tea and those who drank the stuff. One was a prosperous world where the laborers lived in brick houses, sent their children to company funded schools, and their sick to company hospitals. They took good care of the land which was greener than green, and it seemed the land took care of them. They were generally unconcerned about the larger and bleaker world on the other side of the garden fence. Roger's thoughts were interrupted by Kancha's voice. "Your bath water is ready, sir," he said.

"As soon as I finish this drink, Kancha."

The tiger skin hanging from the wall inside the living room suddenly attracted his attention. A phosphorescent blue light was shining from the glass eyes. They forced his mind almost inevitably to thoughts of Alice Newton, the American girl he had met last summer in Rome. Her eyes were blue, he remembered. They had met at a friend's house, and she quickly accepted an invitation to visit India. "I'll probably be hitchhiking through the country," she told him. "Oh! I'll be aichin' too, just whitin' for you," Roger told her.

Although Alice had made known her arrival in Delhi, and was in fact expected in the garden any day, Roger was deliberately shutting his mind off to her. She was quite pretty, he thought, and she was white. What could possibly come of such a fleeting friendship in such an unlikely place as Chirribilli? They would probably drive over to some of the neighboring gardens, take a trip to Darjeeling or Kalimpong, and that would be that. Anything else would be a bonus for both.

"Your bath water is getting cold, sir," Kancha reminded him.

"Thank you, Kancha," replied Roger, slowly rising from the chair. After a slight pause, during which Kancha stood motionless, Roger added softly, "Listen, Kancha, the crickets are clapping their wings tonight."

"Yes, sir," replied Kancha, gravely.

It was while Roger was pampering his body in the hot bath that he decided to send for Chhotki, one of the young pickers he was particularly fond of. Her visits to his bedroom had been suspended during Clarence Ames's unending stay in Chirribilli.

It was Roger's innate English delicacy, his sense of propriety, which prevented him from sleeping with a native girl while his father remained a house guest. But he was prepared to swear to his dying day that Chhotki had the most spontaneous, the most magnificent and passionate contractions he had ever known. In comparison, the women of his kind he had slept with seemed half dead. Perhaps this Alice might be different, he thought wryly from his bath. But he doubted it.

Kancha sent one of the younger servants scurrying to the coolie quarters a short distance away. During the time when Roger finished dinner and settled down with his brandy, Chhotki finished her obligatory bath and sat down to her own meal with the servants. Their dinner was just as silent a ritual as Roger's. By now they knew Chhotki quite well, knew why she had been summoned to the bungalow at that hour. From the day when Chhotki suddenly dropped out of the sky in their midst, they had all been excited and fascinated by her. She was small and diminutive, and so the name Chhotki seemed perfectly appropriate. Nobody knew where she came from. She hardly spoke to anyone the first few months. The imperious laborer whose ward she pretended to be passed her off as an orphaned niece. Nobody believed him, and before long fantastic tales of their sexual perversions began to circulate around the garden. The workers were plainly jealous. Naturally, they were all immensely pleased when they found their manager's sexual needs gradually preempting those of Chhotki's protector whom they referred to as a *goonda* and whom they all hated. Soon they began referring to him behind his back as her pimp.

The servants did not wish to start any indelicate discussions in front of Chhotki for she had a fiery temper as well. They finished their meal quietly and left the bungalow one by one. The silence gave the house a haunted quality, very agreeable to the rumored ghosts of dead planters. Kancha left too, knowing Roger would be safe in their presence. As an added measure of precaution, he made sure the armed guard had arrived and positioned himself behind the bungalow gates.

Chhotki was a little shy tonight. Since she couldn't speak a word of English, Roger could never make up his mind as to whether she was really shy or just being coy. He had discovered her about five months ago, at a time when his reputation as a womanizer had been firmly established. One look at Chhotki, and he decided to give up his wayward ways for good. He found her a permanent job around the bungalow grounds and lavished many gifts on her. Roger's predecessor had warned him, "These coolies are damned touchy about female chastity unless its total surrender is suitably rewarded. Such things as transistor radios, watches, fountain pens, jewelry and of course money work rather well." Roger remembered this advice every time he slept with a local woman. Every time he returned from home leave, he made sure he brought back plenty of goodies for whoever he was courting at the time. He considered the old planter's advice more vital to his existence in India than anything he had picked up during four years of an Economics degree at Trinity College, Cambridge. Nothing else could have secured for him his marvelous sense of freedom on nights such as these, he was sure of that.

Chhotki was resplendent in a clutch of bead necklaces he had given her in days past. Thank God she can't speak English, thought Roger. He knew the beads were her special way of showing appreciation. "Long time no see," he said, welcoming her with a smile. The girl looked back at him with a glow of satisfaction. It was completely genuine, nothing feigned about it.

"The Queen's English!" exclaimed Roger. "What if we can't communicate through it? Our language will be the language of the gods, the language of Eros." With that, he pulled the uncomprehending Chhotki gently by her wrists. She slid beside him on the sofa. Roger poured her a hefty drink. As she cupped her hands around the glass and sipped her drink, Roger admired her glorious body. Even her shining black hair cast a spell upon him tonight. It was braided tightly at the back of her head from where a slender sprig of jasmine spread color and fragrance around her.

The night was memorable, but the next morning began on an ominous note. Roger woke up early to the echoing slogans of a band of young workers who had gathered outside his gates. "We want answers," they shouted. "We'll give up our lives, not honor and self-respect." Still half asleep, Roger found it impossible to make any sense out of it all. Lately, there had been increased political activity around all the local tea gardens. Roger assumed this demonstration was part of some labor grievance whose details would become apparent later in the day. He was about to go back to his bed when Roger thought he heard Chhotki's name being chanted by the demonstrators.

Unable to quite understand the protesters' language, Roger looked questioningly at the dark figure spread voluptuously over his spotless white sheets. Suddenly, Chhotki began to look more bashful than Roger had ever seen her before. She was trying to tell him something. She kept pointing to her naked belly from time to time, but Roger had no idea what she was trying to say. It was only after many curious contortions and gestures that she succeeded in making Roger understand that she was pregnant.

"Oh my God," murmured Roger distastefully. He looked out of the window once more. Directly in front of the gate there stood nearly a hundred coolies. The rabble, he saw, consisted of ordinary line workers. What was unfortunate and dangerous was that they were being led by one of the most formidable coolie *sirdars* in the area. The Nepali guard at the gate stood helplessly by.

By now, Roger had managed to establish in his mind some connection, however speculative, between Chhotki's belly and the disturbance outside. As the initial sense of shock wore off, he decided to confront the situation like a man. He wrapped a silken robe around himself, walked over to the gate, and invited the coolie *sirdar* into his living room. The man could speak a form of English which Roger, after five years in the land, could somehow follow. He listened attentively as the *sirdar* ranted about marriage, society, chastity, and security. Roger lit his pipe, an unfailing ally in moments of crisis. This simple gesture made him look like an intent listener when in fact he was quite distracted and confused.

Quite abruptly, he got up and walked over to the *sirdar*. He put a friendly arm on his shoulder and assured him that he did not expect the men to throw away their honor and self-respect. Most certainly not. Then Roger enquired what was expected of him under the circumstances. The *sirdar* replied that he would have to consult the others. So Roger called them all in.

Those who could not find room inside the house made themselves comfortable in the spacious verandah. The more Roger asked them where they thought his duty lay with regard to Chhotki, the more insistently they wanted to know what his precise intentions were. Although everyone expressed an opinion or two, the situation remained hopeless. They were well and truly bogged down. At half past ten in the morning, Roger Ames did what he thought best in these trying circumstances. He ordered drinks for everyone.

Every available glass was pressed into service. Cups were remorselessly separated from exquisite china saucers. Even delicate crystal wine and liqueur glasses were not spared. Every receptacle was filled to the brim with whiskey and soda and passed round to the men by Kancha and a host of his helpers. While the drama slowly unfolded itself, Chhotki stood in the background. She looked worried. What concerned her was another threatened breach in her pleasant arrangement with Roger. It was bad enough with Clarence Ames around and people taunting her, "So the manager threw you out, huh?" Neither Chhotki nor the coolies ever understood why Roger had suddenly espoused celibacy, so she let it be known it was because of her baby. That helped squelch rumors that Roger was suffering from some sexual disease.

The hours dragged by. Thought grew clouded. Conversation became more and more perfunctory. A solution was nowhere in sight. Little by little the men were getting drunk. At first the women abstained. But the more the men relaxed, the more desirable the women became. Some offered their women a sip or two. They modestly refused at first, but relented when the men grabbed them roughly, drew them close, and touched their lips with fire water. Soon, no one was exempt. As the glow of pleasure descended over all, Roger accurately surmised that what he had done, or intended to do, was now of little consequence to his guests. When he excused himself away from the gathering, his departure from the room evoked no reaction.

Once inside the house, he splashed his tired eyes with water. Chhotki had followed him silently, and now stood watching him from the bathroom door. At a slight nod from Roger, she bolted the bedroom doors from inside. They clung to each other hungrily for a long time. The Englishman needed no words to invite Chhotki to spread out her legs for him for what he imagined would be the last time.

Roger Ames repeated himself twice that afternoon and marveled at his unflagging powers. By now, the men and women sprawled over his living room and verandah had a fair notion of what he was up to behind the bedroom doors. He even succeeded in firing the romantic imaginations of some. In any case, by the time the factory siren went at four in the evening, they had lost all interest in the sensitive matter they had come to discuss with Roger. Sixteen cases of precious imported spirits had been consumed during the day. Now every coolie imagined himself to be Roger Ames. Every woman found herself transformed into Chhotki.

It was time to go home. But few of the men were capable of walking. Luckily, helping hands were extended by curious onlookers who had assembled late in the day to observe the spectacle. Word passed from mouth to mouth, and there were coolies even from gardens far away from Chirribilli. One by one they drifted home, but not before the men had shaken hands with Roger and slobbered sentimentally over his shoulders. They really thought he was the finest tea garden manager in the country, they said repeatedly. In the whole world, said others. Chhotki left with the rest of them. She kept turning back to look at the bungalow long after Roger had disappeared from sight and slumped down in the sofa.

He woke up with a splitting headache after ten that night. Although a dim light shone in the garden, the living room itself lay in total darkness. Vague, indescribable night sounds assured him that the spirits were watching over him. Fumbling in the dark, Roger succeeded in switching on the light. He was startled and then touched to find Kancha sitting against the front door, fast asleep.

"Kancha," Roger called out softly. "You can go home now. I won't be needing any dinner tonight."

Kancha needed a lot of effort to shake off the heaviness in his eyes. As he lifted himself off the ground, Roger spoke to him again. "No, wait Kancha," he said. "I'd like you to pack my bags tonight. I'm going home."

As he read the disbelief in Kancha's eyes, Roger moved his face a little closer and spoke a little louder. "Do you understand? I've been away from home too long." After a pause, he said, "I'm sorry I won't be seeing you again. You helped to make this a home for me too. Tell the driver I want him to stay on tonight. He'll have to drive me to Bagdogra for the early morning flight to Calcutta."

While Kancha went about packing his bags, Roger wrote several letters. One was to his Indian assistant manager, authorizing him to take charge of the garden in his absence. One was to his bank, asking for two substantial payments to be made to Kancha and Chhotki. The last letter consisted of a single sentence addressed to the Chairman, Chirribilli Tea Estates. It read: You can have my fuckin' job. Yours, Roger.

Kancha returned to say that his bags were ready. There was little to pack anyway. The rest would no doubt be shipped later. Most of everything belonged to the company. Roger looked up from the desk where he had been writing the letters. He would have to leave the garden at the crack of dawn to be in time for his flight. He knew Kancha would be waiting for him even at that hour. "Thank you, Kancha," he said. "And good night."

But for the noise from the dark vast stretches outside, the house was in total peace, the spirits at rest. As Kancha searched his mind for something to say, Roger said, "Listen, Kancha. Can you hear the crickets clapping?"

"Yes, sir," replied Kancha, almost inaudibly, as tears rolled down his cheeks.

ছয়

SINCE EARLY morning the black monsoon clouds dissolved in a steady drizzle upon the city. Both Sir Ajoy and Lady Ranu were in a state of shock, and their immediate preoccupations drawn to the level of the trivial. "I don't like it," said Lady Ranu with a frown. She had been standing at the window for a long time, looking not at the rain but the muddy waters swirling in the street below.

Sir Ajoy remained seated at his desk, his face buried in his hands. He didn't respond to his wife. The lights hadn't been lit in his teak-panelled study. Otherwise lavish and elegant, the room was now gloomy and humid. The house was as silent as the street outside. The pendulum in an old grandfather clock clicked softly and monotonously. Raindrops drummed against the glass window. These sounds did not disturb Sir Ajoy's thoughts. Nor did they disturb his wife's single-minded preoccupation with the rising waters outside.

As Lady Ranu stared out of the window, a young man, bare-bodied but for a pair of dark shorts, groped with his feet along the edge of the pavement and heaved open man-hole covers as he found them. As he pulled open the cover in front of her house, she murmured scornfully, "As if that's going to help." Again, she waited for her husband to say something, anything. When he didn't, she walked away from the window. "What are we going to do?" she cried in a choking voice. "How will Vikram live through this nightmare? Will we ever get to the airport on time?"

Sir Ajoy let his hands drop from his face. "What are you worried about?" he asked wearily. "There won't be any planes coming to Dum Dum for a long time today."

Lady Ranu looked helplessly at her husband, then returned to the window. He looked back at her and wondered what was going through her mind. He knew she wasn't thinking of the rain. Perhaps it was the trip to the airport, which she must dread as much as he. He felt angry with himself for having had to weave a story of truths and half-truths for her, as he would have to prepare one for Janaki Devi in Bishnupur. This was too much in their old age. His heart wouldn't be able to endure much more.

He had told Lady Ranu it was something of an accident. But she was as much of a cynic as he to believe in accidents. Sir Ajoy believed that tragedies resulted only from broken promises and betrayals. In public, he wanted to know what the police were doing about Krishna. In his heart he knew there was little they could do. It was no accident that his son had been beaten almost to death, no accident that Krishna had been abducted, probably raped and murdered, no accident that even the blind Malini had been brutalized. Even the water rising in the street was no accident, he thought. For where can you dump the excrement from five million people? No swamp, no river would accept it any more. "We'll choke in our filth in this damned city," he whispered through clenched teeth. He had once prophetically said the same words at a luncheon of the local Rotary Club and impressed his audience no end. "Yes, we must do something about it," they all murmured collectively, gathering round him at the bar for gin and tonic.

There was no need to pretend they were not crying. But the rain did prove an effective cover for the tears in their eyes as Lady Ranu, Sir Ajoy, and a dozen other friends and relatives got to the airport to meet the flight. There were journalists there too, lurking in the background, away from the family group. They would have very little to write, for they were working under guidelines set up by the government. What was the point of following this story when the federal Minister of Information himself had stressed the need for journalistic moderation in the context of the anti-Bengali riots. Even the disappearance of Vikram's wife and a servant boy—and possibly their death — seemed unimportant.

Sir Ajoy drove to Vikram's house in Ballygunge. The bewildered servants stood crying in the shadows. Krishna wasn't there to return their welcome with her smile. Hamid wasn't there to tell them where to go with the luggage. There was no luggage.

Once inside the house, Vikram slumped down in the sofa and closed his eyes. Lady Ranu moved around the room weeping and wringing her hands. The others sat there speechless until Sir Ajoy asked, "What are we to do with Malini?" They would have to wait a few more days for an answer.

It was exactly three days later that Alice turned up at the door to Krishna's house. Failing to find Roger Ames at Chirribilli, she headed back to the hospital where she had first met Malini and Vikram. The hospital superintendent helped her track down Vikram's address. She was grateful for the money Roger's assistant manager willingly loaned to her when she explained her circumstances.

Lady Ranu was sitting with Malini in the family room. She met Alice at the door and ushered her in. She knew nothing of paths that had crossed earlier in the shadow of the mountains. " I am sorry Vikram is not at home just now," said Lady Ranu, trying to sound in control of her voice, "and I'm sorry Krishna isn't here either. We don't know where she is." She could no longer hold back her tears. She burst out crying.

Just then, Alice saw Malini on the sofa, her head turned in their direction, listening intently to her voice.. A barely suppressed scream escaped her lips. She stood there for sometime, clutching herself, trembling, crying, "Oh my God. Oh my God. Oh my God." Then she ran over to Malini, flung her arms around her, and wept freely.

"Do you remember me?" she whispered in Malini's ears. The little girl nodded in reply. Her arms reached out to Alice's face. When she found it, she drew herself up and kissed her over and over again.

Sir Ajoy dropped into the room shortly afterwards. He put his hand on Alice's shoulder and said, "Stay with us as long as you want."

Alice followed Sir Ajoy with Malini in her arms as he took the liberty of showing her Vikram's guest room and hoped she liked it. She thanked him and Sir Ajoy left quietly. Alice sat Malini down on her bed and started to unfasten her shoes.

"I want you to stay with me, Alice," said Malini, clinging to her.

"I will, my little girl," replied Alice, lovingly smoothing her hair.

"Will my Mama come back to me if I pray for her?"

"Yes she will, if we all pray."

Malini sat up in bed. "Shall I pray in your room?" she asked.

"Yes, certainly," said Alice, kissing her longingly on the forehead.

Malini wanted to sleep with Alice. Sir Ajoy decided it was best that she get her father's or her grandma's permission. Later hat evening, the somber mood of the dining table was broken only once when Malini asked if she might sleep in Alice's bed. Vikram said yes, and Malini broke into smiles. But she sensed his mood and said nothing else.

Vikram was totally confused by Alice's presence. "Why is she here and not Krishna," he kept asking himself. He kept brooding while Alice fed Malini and finished her own meal. His eyes narrowed in pain as he let his fingers stray to the tapes that still covered his throbbing head and scratch the scabs that were just beginning to form. Alice saw him and wished she could help him in some way. But she knew she was a stranger, knew where to draw the line.

Vikram had forgotten that Sir Ajoy and Lady Ranu were still around. He was startled when he suddenly found his father's hand on his shoulder. "I want to tell you that the government and the police have promised to do everything to find Krishna quickly," he said. "You'll not let this crush your spirit, will you, Vikram?"

Vikram remained silent. Sir Ajoy continued in his gentle but firm voice. "At other times one tends to detach oneself from such things. You stand on high ground and see the filth swirling way down below. You see it in the morning papers, sucking up little people, men and women who don't really matter. Let this be an object lesson to us. To me, to you, your mother, and others like us. Filth touches us too. Maybe we're only standing with our feet in it. But we're in it just the same as your poor, insignificant people, the people who don't matter."

Speeches again, thought Vikram, as he closed his eyes and said nothing. His mother held his hand in hers before she left for her own home, wanting to comfort him with tears he didn't see. At the door leading out of the room, she mustered enough strength to speak. "We're helpless before the wrath of God, my son," she sobbed. "He has struck us enough blows. Let's hope his anger is now spent. Let's hope he'll return Krishna to us soon."

seven

VIKRAM NEVER liked me much. We had met socially on occasions, but we were never the best of friends. I had a vague suspicion that he never really liked newspapers or people who worked for newspapers. From my friends in the Calcutta press I had heard some details of what had happened and felt I should offer my regrets and sympathy for whatever they were worth. I felt I should drop by. Like everyone else, I held Krishna in the deepest affection. She too, I had met only on social occasions, usually during *Durga Puja*.

I arrived at the house just as Vikram's parents were leaving. Lady Ranu was carefully picking a hibiscus bloom from a plant in the front lawn. Sir Ajoy spotted the sign 'PRESS' stuck behind my windshield. He walked over to me and we introduced ourselves. "Please help us find Krishna," said Sir Ajoy. There were tears in his eyes. I promised I would.

As he walked to his car, Sir Ajoy turned around and said, "I had always thought this could never happen to us. I wonder why. Because we're rich, titled, respectable?" I remained silent and let him go on.

"These things hardly set us apart. The British knighted me possibly because it was too late to do anything to my father. They dumped the title 'Sir' on me because I dumped some of our war-time profits on hospitals and orphanages. Sir, huh! It's more a source of danger than pride. It marks us."

I stayed back after Sir Ajoy and Lady Ranu had left. Most of my time was spent in silence. The servants started locking up for the night. Alice led Malini to Vikram to kiss him good night. She kissed him fondly and mumbled goodbye in his ears. As he watched her leave the room, hand in hand with Alice, I could sense something was going out of Vikram's life. I wasn't quite sure what. He confessed to an emptiness he had never known before. The mood of despondency deepened as the night wore on. He said he wanted to touch Malini, to kiss her and pamper her. But he didn't think he'd ever be able to do that. There was a new fear in his heart, fear of transience, fear of the ruin that had overtaken Krishna's beauty, her fragile body. There was no escape. If it wasn't the hands of Time, it was the hands of Man.

I had never come so close to Vikram. I felt sorry for him. Rahul I knew much better, knew him as a political activist railing against the poverty and inequities he saw around us. We would often meet at the Coffee House on College Street and spend hours dissecting the ills that afflicted our society and the world in general. During the political upheavals of the past eighteen months Rahul had gone underground and then had to flee India. We all knew he would surely be killed if he stayed on in Calcutta.

Eight

THERE WAS only a faint touch of winter in the air the day Rahul landed in Bombay's Santa Cruz Airport. If there was a war on, it seemed to exist on paper. The Russian Mig fighters standing on the edge of the southern runway were real enough, but no more real than the ice cubes colliding in martinis at the Sun-n-Sands Hotel. Here, off-duty servicemen zeroed in on targets nearer home, victims eager to surrender themselves to the nation's finest. Since the stalking hunter and the willing prey both wished to forget the world outside, the Charlie Dorsey Goan Band obligingly filled the main ballroom with the sound of dance music. Even at night, no one paid much attention to the world outside which, blacked out by orders from Delhi, hid nervously behind the crackling leaves of the palm trees.

Contrary to official orders, the moon leapt out of the sea at its appointed hour. It bathed the pleasure seekers on the beach with the pallor of fresh cadavers. This was not the mysterious East of Thomas Cook or American Express. Here was Fort Lauderdale after a power failure, as many of the well-traveled hotel guests remarked. If anyone tried to wrap himself in his mind's peace and quiet, reality swiftly bore down upon him, burying it all under a flood of Burt Bacharach, central air conditioning, room service, and questionable French cuisine.

Rahul wished to see more of the city during the day. He could've done so easily if the Customs hadn't taken three hours to get to his baggage. "What're you bringing these in for?" asked an official, pointing to packets of Kool-Aid and Carnation Instant Breakfast.

"I wanted to give them away to friends," explained Rahul.

"Give them away, eh?" asked the resident narcotics expert. "Well, you can start right here," he said, as he systematically opened every packet.

"So you're an American," sneered the security officer examining his passport. Rahul stopped short of explaining to him that he remained an Indian at heart even though he carried an American passport. He decided it would sound utterly stupid.

A younger and more affable officer now turned his attention towards him. "Does Mr. Nixon suffer from Portnoy's complaint?" he asked, dissolving in laughter.

Rahul stood in silence, feigning embarrassment. He saw no point in saying any more than he had to.

Bombay remained true to his earliest recollections, neither here nor there, a Janus-faced monstrosity playing a deadly game of reviving the past while clutching at the glitter and promise of an unknown future, mixing its hymns to Krishna with 'Lucy in the Sky with Diamonds.' As he had half expected, not all the gods and well-meaning agents could get him on a flight to Calcutta that day. Trying to make it easier for him, they suggested that he try the buffet lunch at the Taj Hotel that afternoon. "After all," said one of the agents, "you're carrying American dollars. You can afford to have a good time."

The hotel was only a few blocks away. Rahul pursued the suggestion up a plush red stairway into an enormous hall echoing to the rhythms of Strauss. Nobody was dancing. Nobody seemed interested. To most of the two hundred patrons, even the food seemed quite incidental. Not to Rahul. The sight of the endless rows of tables laden with colorful foods from East and West awakened in him a ravenous hunger. He moved impatiently past waiters melting with deference, past polite and rude glances, and snatches of conversation punctuated with names of great hotels in Paris, Geneva, Rome, or San Francisco.

There were some tables in the wide corridor outside the hall. It was here that Rahul sat down, beside the glass windows overlooking the Arabian Sea. From where he sat, India Gate was visible less as a gate than a wedge of cheese. The gate did not face him squarely, but merely presented one side to his view. The spectacular arch looked no wider than a narrow passage. Intrepid tourists, heedless of the war, still passed through it, marching down a flight of steps for the cruise to the Elephanta Caves.

Back at the airport, an agent examining his ticket said, "There are dangers you and I don't know of." Then, somewhat more gravely, he asked, "What is the U.S. Seventh Fleet doing in the Bay of Bengal anyway?"

A man hunched over a nearby desk came suddenly to life. "Loading the last consignment of *hilsa* fish for the White House," he said, shaking with laughter.

"No," volunteered someone else. "They can't take the stench of rotten bodies in the Gulf of Tonkin any more." Another perceptive commentator suggested that the Chinese and American cavalry, working in close cooperation, would soon come galloping down the Himalayas and snatch the Pakistan army from the jaws of a humiliating defeat. "The Seventh Fleet is only a diversion," he said, nodding his head wisely.

Rahul slept through the flight to Calcutta. He dreamt that the jet was banking steeply and leveling off towards a different ocean. There was Paris, a limitless spawning ground of pearls, its bright lights shimmering in the night air. London tilted precariously against the window and vanished. Then there was New York, strewn with opals. When he woke up, the Indian Airlines captain was announcing their arrival in Dum Dum. One look through the oval window and Rahul knew nothing had changed.

The airlines bus brought him right into the city. Rahul decided to use public transportation from there, rather than a taxi, to get to his sister's house. As usual, the bus was packed beyond its capacity. Rahul wriggled his body into the solid mass of other bodies and kept eyeing an empty seat marked 'For Ladies Only'. But the solitary woman who sat beside the empty space showed no interest in sharing the seat with a stranger. Without her explicit invitation, Rahul knew he would only be courting a rebuff in asking if he could sit beside her. The bus raced through the traffic, lurching forward of a sudden, then braking with equal suddenness, the latter maneuver having the effect of packing in the passengers even more tightly and miraculously making room for others waiting at the bus stops. Rahul stepped off at one of these.

He picked up his bag and decided to walk over to Krishna's house. It was only a short distance away from the bus stop. With the bag slung across his shoulder, he walked quickly along the streets he knew so well. He drew curious stares, mournful appeals for alms, and even some rude comments. He looked an uncommon traveler and there was no way he could hide this fact. Something about his appearance gave him away as someone living outside the country.

The longer he walked, the more powerfully he realized that something had changed indeed. This was evident from his inner response to the city. He realized the change might be within himself, in his mind, but it was change just the same. There was, for instance, nothing wrong with him physically, yet he was finding it increasingly difficult to walk. It was as if this sprawling city had suddenly grown hills beneath his feet. It was as if he was dragging his body, climbing uphill, his feet slipping under him. He reached out in his mind to the tips of his hands and feet, reassuring his limbs, testing their reflexes. Slightly ahead of him, the narrow asphalt road leveled off or sloped down. He couldn't tell from where he was. And all the while he knew, these ups and downs, these unexpected twists, they all existed in his mind.

He made an effort to shift his thoughts away from his

immediate surroundings. He succeeded, but his mind reminded him immediately of the pain plucking at the tendons in his feet. Rahul looked up at the sky waiting for him at the top of the road, bright, clear, of no single color in particular. Several indefinable shades blended together, so that the sky looked simply pale. His thoughts bounced off it, and finding the certitude of the street more dependable, renewed their questioning of his feet.

Rahul stopped, rose slowly on his toes, and felt the pain climb to the calves and to the muscles in his thighs. The sunlight fell over some of the houses, avoided some of the others, each a prisoner held in place between neighbors, unchanging from day to day, year to year. It's just the inhabitants who come and go, he thought, as he looked up and saw a mother and son on a balcony. He couldn't remember them living there three years ago. The boy sat with a red blanket draped over his legs. He waved at Rahul, but something prevented him from waving back, from establishing the boy's face as anything more than a blur.

He thought he knew what the trouble was. Perhaps he was not alive any more. This suspicion grew stronger the closer he came to Krishna's house. Again, he couldn't remember which way the road went up ahead. The rows of houses radiated away from him left and right. The sky came down with its pale vastness on the houses and the road. It was winter. But those couldn't be trees pointing up from the children's park in front. Maybe they were not trees, just men and women.

A few yards from Krishna's house, his feet simply refused to move any more. The windows of the upper floor received the last of the daylight while the rest of the house lay engulfed in shadows. At that place and hour, the windows of the upper floor were little pools of light standing fast against the creeping dusk, the trim white frames dividing each window into four squares of silver.

Rahul was drawn by a slight movement behind one of the windows. When the movement stopped, he could see the outline of a face. Only the face seemed to catch the sun. The rest of the body remained in darkness. As if to make it impossible for him to recognize the face, a flaw in the glass distorted it to a frightening ugliness. The face seemed to dissolve in the light. One eye grew to an immense size and lodged itself in one corner of a giant head. The other eye melted and disappeared altogether. The mouth, or rather one corner of the mouth, drew itself out like pliant glass and dipped delicately to one side, as if waiting for the next breath through the blower's tube.

The face moved. It drew closer to the glass. As the person moved away from the window and the flaw in the glass created another hideous bulge on the face, there was nothing to suggest that the person on the other side had recognized Rahul. He kept standing in front of the house, looking up. Even if his feet would let him, Rahul felt he would be making a mistake in crossing his sister's threshold, now that she was no longer there. Of his own free will, he had made himself a stranger to his people. Could he reverse that and assert his earlier ties so easily?

Krishna would've welcomed him with open arms. He was not so sure of Vikram. There seemed no point in walking through the gate and pressing the doorbell. Rahul turned and started to walk away. He felt no pain any more.

If he had waited just a little longer, he might have discovered that the person behind the glass was Alice. She saw him, recognized him, and waited only because she couldn't believe her eyes. She expected him to walk into the house. By the time she came down to the road below, he was gone.

She took a few uncertain, frantic steps on the road until a purple, sausage-shaped balloon floated in front of her as if from nowhere. She looked up instinctively at the sky. Pale as before, the sky offered no clues to the ownership. The balloon escaped her hands and came to rest at her feet. But only for a moment. There was a slight breeze, and trapped in it, the balloon jumped about like a fat pigeon hesitating between food and fright.

"Thank you, lady," said an unseen voice. "Could I have the balloon back, please?"

It was a child's voice. Alice stopped in her tracks, trying to place it without turning her head away from the road.

Another voice said, "I'm here." A woman's face, gaunt and ravaged by age, looked down from a window. "I'll come down and get it."

It was for her son, she said. He was a cripple, been that way from birth. Alice returned her the balloon and walked back distractedly to the house.

Nine

I was not prepared for Rahul's unexpected return to Calcutta. So, when Rahul called me at home one evening, shortly after my visit with Vikram, I was amazed. I arranged to meet with him two days later, surprised over the name of the hotel my servant passed on to me.

Rahul seemed perfectly at home in a grimy, smelly hotel room on Ezra Street. He was surrounded by piles of newspapers and magazines, and seemed quite unconcerned about the endless commotion outside his window

"So what brought you back so unexpectedly?" I asked.

"I was going crazy in America," he answered.

"So what's new?" I asked. "You've always been a lunatic. Did you come back to get killed?"

"No, I'm back because of Krishna. I feel devastated."

I didn't know what to tell Rahul, or how to ease his pain. So I reached out for the stained and grimy cup of tea one of the hotel boys had just brought to the room and planted before me on a beat-up table.

Directly below the window, facing the street, was the hotel kitchen. Till the early hours of the morning, it sent up the smell and sounds of mouth watering kebabs and egg rolls. Rahul confessed he had been walking down to the kitchen every few hours to satisfy his hunger. In the process, he had endeared himself to just about everyone in the hotel. It didn't matter to the Muslim hotel owner that Rahul was a Hindu. What impressed him more was the fact that Rahul had just stepped off a plane from America.

"My own city refuses to recognize me and my hotel for the quality of my food and service," said the owner to one of his regular customers, "but my patrons come from foreign lands where they know my real worth." The customer was unimpressed at first when the man pointed to Rahul and announced that here was a gentleman from America. "But he looks like one of us," said the customer.

"Looks can be very deceiving," said the owner, nodding his head wisely. Turning to Rahul, he said, "A few years ago we even had an American guru spend two months in my hotel, in the very room you're now occupying." Then, pointing to a tube well standing on the sidewalk in front of the hotel, he added, "But nobody ever saw him take a bath." Later, as if to prove his claim, the man rummaged through his cash-box and produced a U.S. dollar bill on which was written — 'To my friend, Salim Ali, from A. Ginsberg'.

The invisible war asserted itself through the daily headlines. Again, the city reflected nothing of it. Calcutta seemed preoccupied only with itself. There was some talk of the millions of refugees herded into camps only twenty miles from the city. But like the war, they too were invisible. At least one couldn't see them unless one drove for miles. It wasn't a pleasant drive, hardly worth the stench and squalor waiting at the other end.

Rahul was a bit diffident about asking the proprietor, a Muslim, what he thought of the war. The man himself brought up the topic on the second day of his stay. "I suppose," he said, "you've come to write about the war and the refugees like those white-skins with their expensive cameras in the Grand and the Great Eastern Hotels." Salim Ali ignored Rahul's protests about not being a war correspondent. "Let me tell you," he continued, lowering his voice a little, "it's all humbug."

Rahul looked at him curiously. "You mean there isn't a war?" he asked.

"No," replied Salim Ali quite firmly. "Ayub Khan and the Pakistani army needed some whores, so they went after them. Mujib's men also need the same things, so they end up whoring in Calcutta. It's all to do with women, see?"

Before Salim Ali started boasting to his customers that he too had a war correspondent in his hotel, Rahul made it clear to him that he had no business in the city, that he was going home to his village in Bishnupur up north.

"That's pretty close to the border, isn't it?" asked Salim Ali slyly.

"Yes," replied Rahul. "But it's the village next to it that's smack on the border. Hazariganj, it's a largely Muslim village. I've no business at the border."

"I remember," said Salim Ali, "it was beyond Hazariganj that we crossed over from West to East Bengal after the partition. There used to be a pretty village on the other side. It's name was Hasnabad. I think it was December, ninety forty seven, when they tore up the tracks between Hasnabad and Hazariganj. It was such a long time ago." Salim Ali sounded sad. "It was to keep us, Muslims and Hindus, apart from each other, was it not?" He nodded thoughtfully. "But blood runs thicker than religion. That's what I think."

"I don't know," said Rahul, turning his face away from the smoke rising from the kitchen fires.

I knew Rahul was headed for Bishnupur. "This time there's no reason for you to come," he said to me. "I guess it's my father still pushing me on, testing me, pushing me to the brink." I wanted to go with Rahul, but he was insistent. "There's no need for you to take on this burden," he said firmly.

When he reached Bishnupur the next morning, Rahul was surprised to see a mountain of construction material lying alongside the platform. "What's this all about?" he casually asked the station master.

"You must be a stranger here," said the man. "All that stuff is for the Railwaymen's Convention due to begin here in a few weeks. The Railway Minister will himself preside over the closing session. I'm afraid you'll hardly be able to recognize our little village in a week or two. First the convention, then the annual fair."

"I thought the fair was usually held earlier," said Rahul.

"That's true," replied the station master, "but this year it has not been the same. The phony war, you know, and the refugees."

"And Sambhu Narain's plays?" asked Rahul.

"All that's in the past," replied the station master with a wistful smile, "even though I think Sambhu Narain's back. Suddenly turned up one day just like that, after his daughter went missing. Many travelers from the north say they've seen him in the company of holy men. He comes and goes as he pleases. Speaks very little."

"And what about Janaki Devi?" asked Rahul.

"You ask too many questions, stranger." The station master had grown suspicious. He stepped closer to Rahul to take a good look at his face. "Who may you be?" he asked.

"I'm Rahul Chaudhury. Sambhu Narain's son."

The station master gasped in disbelief. His spectacles slid down to the tip of his nose. "Oh my God!" he exclaimed, embracing Rahul and starting to cry. "Your mother's a very holy person or you wouldn't have been sent here in her hour of need." He released Rahul and glanced around him fearfully. He whispered to him to follow him into the ticket office for it was not safe to be standing where they were.

The train blew its whistle and painfully pulled out of the station as Rahul and the station master walked the length of the platform and entered the modest station building. The old man promptly secured the ticket window and bolted the door from inside. Rahul could barely hide his impatience as he asked him what was going on. The man collapsed into a chair and said he had a long story to tell. But he would try to be brief with Rahul.

He began by reminding Rahul that his brother's death and Sambhu Narain's disappearance left Janaki Devi totally helpless in Bishnupur. The people in the village were always ready to help his mother, he said. Unfortunately, before they knew what was happening, the local Congress boss had moved into her home. Chanchal Sircar, the very man the government had sent to Bishnupur as a social worker. Rahul admitted he had never met him. The station master lowered his voice still further and declared emphatically that there was no truth to what many detractors were whispering behind their backs. The truth simply was that Janaki Devi welcomed Chanchal into her home as a son, only to be cheated out of everything. Sambhu Narain's recent return had not made the slightest difference.

"He lives in a world apart. We've watched this with pain and anguish, but Chanchal's a powerful man and nobody dares say anything in public. Thank God you've finally come home." He wiped away his tears and clasped Rahul's hands in his.

A passing thought took hold of the old man. He asked Rahul what he himself had been up to all these years. Rahul replied that he had been studying abroad, which wasn't such a good answer because the station master promptly asked if he had forgotten how to write in his mother tongue. Rahul had little choice but to inform his inquisitor that he had been studying in a monastery, a Buddhist monastery, totally secluded. The man seemed satisfied and impressed by Rahul's explanation. He nodded his head in silent understanding.

Rahul was a bit uncertain as to what might be expected of

him in Bishnupur. The station master wasted no time in telling him quite sharply that the rascal Chanchal had usurped his rightful position. It was up to him to recover what was legally his, up to him to take charge of the Chaudhury household once more.

Rahul had no intentions of telling the old man that the last thing he wanted to do was take charge of his family estate. But he did enquire about his mother, whether she had given up everything without a murmur of protest.

"Without protest," he said. "Whatever interest she might've had, it was all gone when Krishna disappeared. I've seen her at the station from time to time. She never complains. Not even to Durga Chakravartty, the priest, who feels just as outraged by events and circumstances and sees her much more frequently over prayers."

Janaki Devi wasn't in Bishnupur at the time. "I think she left for Calcutta sometime last week," recalled the station master. "She goes there often to stay with Malini, your sister's little girl. Poor girl. But Sambhu Narain might turn up any time, if he isn't home at this time. There's no telling when."

Perhaps he ought to go home and wait for his father's return, said Rahul. But the station master cautioned him to be careful and not to mention their conversation to anyone.

Rahul wasn't at all prepared for the surprise that awaited him at home. Chanchal couldn't be more cordial, more deferential. "Your mother has wept day and night these three years," he said, "waiting for your return, and now waiting for your sister's return. She has wept and prayed. So have we. These have been very difficult years, but we've done our best and hope you'll approve."

Chanchal said his mother might be home any day, for she seldom stayed in Calcutta more than a couple of weeks at a time. But when Rahul asked about his father, Chanchal looked troubled. "He lives in a world of his own," he replied, in words Rahul had heard before. "Comes and goes when he pleases."

Then he turned to Rahul and asked what wonderful adventures he had had these past few years. Rahul knew he would have to deal with such questions before long, but he had made up his mind to say nothing. He was saved for the moment as there suddenly appeared a slight, frail man who fell at his feet. The prostrate figure was paying his respects, but Rahul stepped back in embarrassment. When he saw it was the old servant, Panchu, he bent down and lifted him gently off the ground. "You've grown so big, master," said Panchu, trying to hold back his tears.

Word spread quickly through the village. People began to drop by almost immediately and continued to do so all day long. With Sambhu Narain having given up control over his earthly possessions and ties, the return of his son held the suggestions of a new order in the house, if not the entire village. The many tragedies that visited the family in recent years touched every heart in Bishnupur. But neither the priest nor the postmaster or the grocer repeated anything of what the station master had said to Rahul, which bothered him.

Many came out of simple curiosity, to see a man who had traveled across the seas, the one solitary detail of his recent history Rahul had been compelled to disclose to his visitors. "Is it true," asked a young boy "that in America they can turn donkeys into horses, unlike here?"

It had always been an exclamation of despair and disgust in Bengal to say you couldn't change one into the other, that fools would remain fools. Rahul stopped laughing and was about to explain that Americans were indeed very clever. But the boy's father yanked the lad by his ear out of the room for his impertinence, and so saved Rahul the need to champion American wisdom.

Chanchal looked after him well, making sure he was fed well and often. He rarely left his side, especially when visitors were around. In spite of all this care and attention, Rahul came down with high fever on the third night of his stay. Like on a previous occasion, he thought he was going to die. At least, he was certain he had passed out in the middle of the night during one of his frequent sprints to the outhouse on the far side of the courtyard. He had no idea whether it was day or night when he finally regained his senses.

As he stirred out of his sleep, his head groggy, his fevered eyes could only see fields that stretched uninterrupted behind the house for miles. There still wasn't enough light to bring into focus the trees silhouetted outside his window. Drunk with dew, they squatted low against the sky, sucking the colors from the horizon's edge.

A long time passed before Rahul heard the sparrows chirping outside. Uncertain and undecided, they scattered from the treetops like dust in the wind, then shot back just as suddenly to settle in the canopied trees. As they alternated between sudden fright and serenity, visible one moment and mere voices the next, Rahul knew it was morning. The morning still held some terror for the birds, terror from which they found shelter in the leaves and branches. He imagined he felt like the birds, felt his world descending upon him like a bird of prey, its eyes full of satanic joy, tempting him, humiliating him.

Rahul drew his quilt closer against his body and hoped he was free at last of the uncontrollable shivering which had seized him the night before. The fever had left him now, and invisible hands seemed busy wringing the sweat off his body. He badly needed a change of clothes. Those he had on were almost as wet as the quilt. Getting up seemed to require so much effort that he decided to wait a little longer, frightened that the trembling might return the moment he stepped off the bed. Malaria, dengue fever, enteric, names of familiar diseases passed through his mind as he set about trying to diagnose his symptoms. Even if he were to write himself a prescription, he hadn't the faintest idea where medicines might come from in a village like Bishnupur. Finally, he was pleased to leave the problem in the hands of a Dr. Bagchi whom the resourceful Panchu brought in to see him later that morning.

Dr. Bagchi chatted happily. His fees never varied. Two rupees for a prescription, two rupees for a simple examination, two rupees for a medical certificate to justify almost anything. But to charge money for examining Sambhu Narain's son would be nothing short of disgraceful. Having made this lofty statement, he pinched Rahul, looked into his eyes, made him breathe deeply, patted his tummy, and finally asked, "What did you eat last night?"

Smiling weakly, Rahul admitted he had eaten just about everything that had been placed in front of him. The same with the meal before that, and the one before that. The doctor interrupted him, saying he would now have to pay for his weakness. "Nothing but barley water for the next forty eight hours," he said, emphasizing every word with a wagging finger as if he was admonishing a child.

Dr. Bagchi left promising to send some pills later in the day. Panchu dutifully started bringing Rahul his barley water every few hours. Chanchal dropped in too, enquiring how he was feeling, asking if he needed anything to make himself comfortable. "There must've been one bad shrimp," he said thoughtfully, "enough to knock a grown man out." Chanchal proceeded to abuse Panchu for not examining the day's shopping more carefully. Panchu kept his head bowed and listened to Chanchal's tirade in silence.

"I must leave you for a few hours," said Chanchal eventually. "I have to finish some business in the village. I'm sure I'll find you much better when I return."

As soon as Chanchal had stepped out of the house, Panchu came and knelt down beside Rahul's bed. "You must leave this place as soon as you can," he said. The servant looked sick with worry. "It's not safe for you here."

In spite of his weakness, Rahul started to laugh. "You must've had more than your share of *ganja* this morning, Panchu," he said. "Who would want to harm me here, in my own home?"

Panchu was adamant, certain that someone had put something in his food the night before. Even though he told Panchu he was speaking utter nonsense, a tiny grain of suspicion remained in Rahul's mind. Sounding desperate,

Panchu implored with him to go away for a few days at least, perhaps to Siliguri, and return when Janaki Devi was back.

Rahul began to think it was not such a wild idea after all. He needed some dry clothes right away and some warm clothes as well. It could get quite chilly in the northern parts of the province. Panchu told him not to worry, for all of Sambhu Narain's clothes were still around. Rahul could happily take whatever he wanted. But he had to hurry. There was no time to lose.

For the first time in many years, the irony of his immediate needs came home to Rahul. Clothes, money, personal safety. There was a time when he would've scorned such concerns. Property he would most certainly have banished from his scheme of things. If he had any need for money, the need was confined to a world of cigarettes, coffee, and bus tickets. As a student, his mother never begrudged him whatever it all added up to. Sambhu Narain didn't seem to care.

How he loathed his father's world, his pretensions, his naive conniving, his subtle self-pity. Now he hated him more for having abandoned his mother. Poor father, nothing to remember him by except for all those despicable things he valued.

The one nice thing Rahul remembered about his father was a single image of Sambhu Narain towering above his head, tall and sturdy as a slim birch. Everything else was fading. Trying to capture these forgotten images was like walking into a deserted town. Only the empty shells of buildings, but no life one could relate to. But there was one image he was beginning to remember, the image of a winter's day, and little Rahul walking hand in hand with his father.

It came back to him now. Every time he ran, running being his favorite mode of relaxation, it was this single image that took hold of his mind for long periods. He would have loved to drive it out of his mind, if only he knew how. Every time he looked back over the hump that separated their lives, he was still walking with his hand in his father's. He could hear his sneakers going pitter-patter over the glazed asphalt, still straining to keep pace with his father's enormous strides as they stepped out of a glorious avenue and wandered south along the river.

How beautiful their house in Calcutta used to be then. One walked into the avenue as soon as one stepped out of the gates. There was a strange pleasure merely in walking in and out of those gates. It mattered little where one was walking to, and upon what errand. Rahul couldn't have been more than four years old then. He found it strange that he couldn't remember other occasions when he and Sambhu Narain must at least have been physically close to one another if nothing else. Something happened as he grew older. Could it be that, at a certain point, they had each made a conscious choice to go their separate ways. Or was it that he seemed merely to be retracing his father's steps, a little behind in time. Like his father, was he too picking up society's worn out hand-me-downs along the way?

He had no doubt his father had once belonged to a class one could describe as the elite. There was always a great deal of adulation heaped upon him. Most of all, he was a hero to his family and relatives, the one son of his father who had broken away from his rustic beginnings in the ancestral village of Bishnupur and gained a degree of prominence and respect in the city. Sambhu Narain's two brothers died in Bishnupur even before their father, one of smallpox, the other of typhoid. So, it was left to Sambhu Narain to present himself as the one shining beacon to his far-flung relatives. With the looks of a fairy-tale prince, pretty secretaries slowed down as they walked past his glass-walled office during the day, hoping to catch his eyes or, better still, elicit some trivial request or irrelevant enquiry. His colleagues from the press, who looked derelict to the last man, reviled him for his outward appearance and, while they sipped their acrid coffee or cheap whiskey, regretted that the man didn't have more talent. But within the family, Sambhu Narain's excellence remained unchallenged. Your father wrote this, your father would never wear it, your father wouldn't be seen alive with him. Such were the absolute canons with which Rahul grew up. They came less from his mother than from his relatives. At the time, it never occurred to him to question them. Until they finally parted one day, everyone thought he was destined to remain faithful to his father's stylish ways.

When Sambhu Narain moved to Bishnupur in nineteen fifty nine, there was great consternation within the family. A change was coming over him, and he seemed indifferent to what people thought. He still dressed well, carrying around his hardy British suits. They showed up each year at the end of summer when it was time to get them aired. They looked so limp and sad, they reminded Rahul of the feeling of emptiness one felt backstage at the end of a play. Like the first year in college when he worked with the student production of 'Julius Caesar.' He had the mindless task of sorting out the *dhoties* that passed for togas, the wooden swords and the papier-mâché helmets, after everyone had gone home. It was dreadful work. He had the time of his life accounting for everything, especially on the final day when Caesar's ink-stained mantle and his parchment will couldn't be found. They suspected some poor servant had made off with the mantle, but who would steal Caesar's will? Who would want to wear his father's old clothes, Rahul asked himself, as he prepared to go through Sambhu Narain's possessions with Panchu.

Still somewhat weak, he moved slowly into the room where Panchu prepared to exhibit his master's former wardrobe with all the pride and flair he could muster. An enormous steel trunk unexpectedly disgorged the old British suits. Sambhu Narain had visited London in nineteen thirty nine, purchased four Seville Row suits for a fortune, and nursed them through repairs and alterations for the next twenty years. His sartorial standards having once been established, Sambhu Narain remained secretly contemptuous of Indian tailors for the rest of his life. As far as Rahul knew, only one tailor, an arthritic old man by the name of Farookh Rahman, ever found favor in his eyes. One single tailor in a land of five hundred million people! When questioned on this subject, Sambhu Narain replied, "That's not at all surprising. Out of every million Indians, how many bother to dress? Not more than a hundred, I'd say. And out of this hundred, perhaps one person knows what it is to dress with taste. Given this limited clientele, if there were others of the caliber of Farookh Rahman they'd all starve."

Rahul saw his father as a man of clashing contradictions, a

man who had failed to find his place in time. He looked down at the English suits and saw the patches, worn and shiny, and other spots that had been skillfully darned. As the smell of mothballs and *neem* leaves rose to his nostrils, it occurred to him that there was one towering relationship in his father's life which seemed to dwarf all others. The fruitful and steady association — Rahul even thought of it as a collaboration — between Sambhu Narain and Farookh Rahman. Together, they had guided the English suits through two decades of structural change, working their way past fluctuating lapels and uncertain cuffs. Somehow, the thought appealed to Rahul. Happy in the thought that Farookh Rahman had indeed played his part well, Rahul picked up one of the darker suits. He assured Panchu that was all he'd need to tide him over the winter.

As he led Rahul back to his room, Panchu said, "You know something, a young man came looking for you a few months ago. Chanchal wouldn't let him inside the house so he couldn't speak to your mother. He threatened to beat him up if he ever caught him on the Chaudhury estate again. He has changed a lot, but I'm sure that was the boy servant your sister took in about the time you went abroad."

Rahul wasn't sure if he had heard Panchu correctly. His face lit up with excitement. "Do you remember exactly when he came here?" he asked in a quiet voice.

Panchu couldn't be sure. Maybe two months, maybe three, he ventured. With that, he turned to leave the room, saying he would prepare a flask of barley for Rahul to take with him on the train.

"I won't be taking a train, Panchu. Instead, could you get

me a bicycle?"

"You're in no shape to ride a bicycle," protested Panchu indignantly. But he soon relented, promising to get the bicycle as long as Rahul wouldn't leave without the barley water.

Ten

THE DAYS passed slowly for Alice. When it rained it reminded her of home where she stared out of her bedroom window for hours at a line of fir trees wearing dew drops on their branches. As soon as a drop grew too heavy and tore itself away, another speck of moisture slid into its place until, bloated and ripe, it too fell to the ground. Alice's eyes leapt from tree to tree, from branch to branch, as she chased these dancing points of light in her backyard. She was sad that monsoon torrents never gave a chance to such playfulness.

In November, it felt like spring in Massachusetts. Alice imagined the little buds of yellow, red and green beginning to cluster around the branches she knew so well, the rents in the icy crust covering the fields melting away each day. People noticed for the first time the lifeless stubble spread its brown shadow over the waking land. The distant trees looked like slender giants groping blindly over the land, their outstretched arms touching the roof of the sky, trailing a crazy jungle of veins and arteries torn out of summer, stiffened by the cold air. There was no such drama in her first Indian winter.

The American Consulate was ready to help her get back home any time she wanted. They knew vaguely of her problems. Roger Ames, now a resident of the United States, imagined she was having a whale of a time in India. It was Malini who held Alice back. The two had become inseparable. Deep in her heart, she felt a need to balance the pain inflicted on her against the kindness she had found so unexpectedly from Vikram and his family. Just about everyone accepted her as a member of the family. Only Vikram's unpredictable moods surprised her from time to time. They might even have proved annoying, but she could never allow herself any ill feeling towards those who had welcomed her so warmly, those who had suffered so greatly. She understood how Vikram felt. He was so different from Rahul. So controlled, and yet so vulnerable.

The police came up with no information on Krishna, or Hamid for that matter. Vikram found time to think of many things during those months without Krishna. He prepared himself to examine many issues he felt important, things like his continued involvement in a job which paid him handsomely in return for minimal responsibilities. Maybe he ought to look for a change, a job more meaningful. He even began to consider migrating to Australia or North America. He agreed with the certainty in the minds of many of his friends that the city was headed for a bloodbath and eventual extinction. For Malini's sake, he ought to get out while he could. There was another matter beginning to bother him. The less he thought of Krishna, the more he thought of Alice. Both thoughts filled him with dread.

Some mornings he would sit back for hours at the breakfast table, reading and re-reading the newspaper, pouring himself endless cups of tea. He suspected he did that only to provoke a reaction from Alice. But not this morning. Today there was an important visitor who couldn't be kept waiting too long. Vikram shaved and got dressed well before his guest arrived.

"Good morning, Mr. Jhunjhunwala," he said, walking into the family room. "I hope you didn't have to wait too long."

"Good morning, Vikram. I hope I didn't wake you up too early." The wily millionaire was always courteous.

"No, Mr. Jhunjhunwala. But this is such a lovely day, I could lie in bed and look out of the window all morning."

"You should get some more sleep. You don't look well at all."

"More sleep, and keep you waiting longer?"

"I always manage to keep myself amused." He put aside a magazine he had picked up from the table and came to the point. "I've come to see you on important business."

He needn't have stressed the obvious. Vikram had guessed it the moment he was informed of the visitation. He now prepared himself for the worst.

"I've just come back from Delhi yesterday. I had gone in connection with the new contract to supply tea to the armed forces. I have tendered for the business and I want it badly." He spoke with the air of a man accustomed to having his own way. "Now listen carefully, Vikram. I'll buy the tea from your company's gardens if need be. But I must have the supply and distribution. Your company must not go directly to the government."

Vikram listened in silence. He had anticipated this problem as soon as his company began eyeing the government contract. For some reason, the Chairman seemed quite prepared to overlook an important fact that Jhunjhunwala was among the biggest customers of several other divisions of the company. "We'll worry about it as and when our tender clashes with Jhunjhunwala's," said the Chairman, flatly dismissing the possibility. "We'll cross that bridge our own way when the time comes."

Jhunjhunwala continued, "Your man Hudson seems bent on trying to rub me up the wrong way." Vikram nodded understandingly. "Other members of our community have been complaining about the same trouble with him. Do you think he is trying to impress the Board for some kind of a reward?"

"Maybe," ventured Vikram. "He has had a fantastic career, you know. Chalked up an unbelievable sales record while based in Singapore."

"Personally, I think he's a fraud. Haridasbhai mentioned to me that he was quite happy to back down from his traditional commission rates after he had arranged for Hudson to have stab at Pershad's wife. You've met Pershad, haven't you?"

"Yes I have," replied Vikram drily. More than Haridasbhai's commercial manager, he remembered his wife, a statuesque female of overwhelming voluptuousness.

"Of course, I don't blame Hudson," laughed Jhunjhunwala. "Not when one has a dried-up prune like Sylvia for a wife. I myself sit with my legs crossed in the presence of Kummoo Pershad." They laughed and thumped the table over these obscenities for a moment. Then it was business again. "Tell me, how can I get him to name his price?"

"Why don't you have him over for dinner?" asked Vikram, for want of a better suggestion.

The visitor seemed to take no offence. He tapped his fingers on the table. "I have a better idea than that," he said. "I've been able to lay my hands on some nice French films. What say you we ask him over to the Miniature Theatre one evening? These are rare films. We should be able to straighten this out over drinks afterwards. I want you to arrange this, Vikram."

"Do you think you could leave me out of the film show?" he asked. He found little to interest him in the kind of bizarre sex he knew would be splashed across the screen. Of course, there might be the odd gangster and the usual murders. But basically, he knew it was always an ode to coitus. 'Coitus, coitus, O curious coitus.' Vikram never forgot this haunting line from one of his first blue movies, garbed like a Greek classical tale, in the Miniature Theatre.

Mr. Jhunjhunwala would brook no refusal. "Certainly not, Mukherjee," he said firmly. "These are good educational films. Teach you a thing or two." He winked conspiratorially at Vikram.

"Please Mr. Jhunjhunwala," Vikram pleaded, "I don't think it'll be proper for me to be present during any part of the discussions. I simply don't feel up to it."

Jhunjhunwala slapped Vikram heartily on the back. "I like you, Mukherjee," he said. "You're the only decent Bengali in this fucking city. Don't let yourself be brow-beaten by these Britishers. We could snuff the buggers out of here like this." He added a menacing gesture for emphasis. "We let them stick around because they are fair game. Besides, this way we don't have to screw only our own kind. Piss on their jobs. Join me any day you want. And make four times as much money as you've been making."

Vikram smiled ruefully. "Thank you, Mr. Jhunjhunwala, for your kind offer," he said. While Vikram was repelled by his foul mind, he could not deny the man his infinite magnetism. Vikram was directly responsible to his own firm for a large slice of Epic Enterprises' profitable account. But for Jhunjhunwala, he would still have remained a struggling assistant in the legal department. While he grudged him the gratitude that was his due, Vikram derived some comfort from the knowledge that he had always managed to keep Krishna away from his sphere of contamination. By and large, he felt inclined to shrug off the few annoying and sometimes childish obligations of his present job.

In a final burst of expansiveness, Jhunjhunwala confided a little more in Vikram. "The Commerce Secretary in New Delhi was a hard nut to crack. He said he was a public servant, detached and impartial. His sole interest lay in obtaining the most favorable terms for his government. Slowly, I pried out of him the details of Hudson's offer. It was like peeling an onion. Naturally, he was convinced that was by far the best. I had a fair idea what formed the basis of his convictions. I was certain Hudson could never have offered him anything more than ten. I offered him fifteen thousand, payable in sterling.

The fool hesitated. I knew then he had already pocketed the money from Hudson. So I suggested this compromise. Since he's still accepting bids on the direct business, I asked him to give your company twenty percent of that. Now I must get Hudson to resubmit his earlier tender for a smaller volume on more restricted terms."

"Sounds ingenious to me."

Mr. Jhunjhunwala was irrepressible. "I don't know why the government keeps people like Mr. Tiwari on its payroll," he said. "Why waste the poor taxpayer's money when, between us, we businessmen could keep every one of the nation's civil servants happy. And they'd earn infinitely more too."

"And be more efficient?" asked Vikram, out of politeness.

"Right." Jhunjhunwala stood up to leave. "Well, bye bye, Vikram," he said. Then, with something of a leer in his eyes, he added. "I see you've got a very nice governess for your daughter. I thought they had priced themselves out of the market. Do bring her over one day."

"I can't get her to go out at all," said Vikram haltingly. "She has a mind of her own. She's very independent."

"But I remember seeing her at Clarence's party," said the man slyly.

"Oh yes, I remember. That time my mother had insisted she go, saying she and my father would look after Malini. It was supposed to be an intimate gathering, hardly a party. You know that."

Jhunjhunwala walked slowly to hide his limp. As he stepped into his car he patted Vikram half affectionately, half patronizingly. "Don't worry, Mukherjee, I understand. By the way, any news of Krishna? We miss her so."

Vikram didn't have to answer the question. Mr. Jhuhjhunwala was in the car, the door shut, and the car was on its way before he could utter a word.

The inevitable party in Jhunjhunwala's house was not long in turning up. Alice received a special invitation. She was excited over the party but pretended desperately to seem otherwise. She dressed with care and chose, at Vikram's insistence, a brilliant purple *sari* from the many Krishna treasured, one with massive flowers woven with gold threads. She looked exquisite.

At the party, the men eyed her appreciatively and, drunk with hope, plotted their progress towards her through the crowd. Alice was herself awed by the vivid *saris* trailing orange, crimson, blue, and every color under the sun. Her fingers longed to touch and feel the rich chiffons, silks from the temples of the south worn only once by the deity's vestals, and magnificent brocades from Benares. Vikram was always at her side, guiding her through the rustling fabrics and a pirate's dream of diamonds, sapphires, and rubies.

Many affectations and pleasantries later, they found themselves standing before steaming platters of Peshawar rice swimming in the misty aroma of tender lamb and saffron, sizzling kebabs grilled to a glorious brown, monstrous shrimps fresh from the Bay of Bengal, bowls of creamy curds and custards. There was all the sensuousness of ancient Dionysian rites in the sprawling garden lit with a thousand lamps of blue and red, artfully concealed in trees and bushes. Mr. Jhunjhunwala was polite and courteous, but too preoccupied with other priorities to offer Alice more than cursory compliments.

At other times, Alice would've been quite content to stay at home, reading aloud to Malini, asking her questions, inwardly thrilling to her answers. She began to remind her more and more of Susan back home, whom she hardly missed, knowing she would be well looked after by Ginny. They got along fine.

At the beginning, Vikram suffered some doubts about the propriety of being seen with Alice at parties, the one at Jhunjhunwala's being truly her first big one. But when she started receiving personal invitations, there was little he could do except hope that their hosts weren't deliberately trying to set them up.

Fortunately for Alice, the Christmas season was about to come to an early end. She was quite happy about it. The social whirl in Calcutta ebbs perceptively around this time. After the first few rounds, Alice knew the recurring faces, the favorite subjects of conversation, the people to avoid, and the people to snub. She even learned to tell the extent of adulteration in the Scotch by looking at her host's face. In fact, she could even tell the exact time when large scale adulteration began. It had something to do with the speed of service and the degree of the waiters' inebriation.

During all this time, Alice hardly ever visited the Swimming Club, or the two golf clubs, or attended any of the get-togethers arranged by expatriate wives to amuse themselves in the name of charity. On the rare occasion when they met, they took pains to assure Alice they were socially her superior. It just so happened that their uneven paths had somehow managed to cross.

"George came back from Washington the other day," announced a formidable banker's wife at one of the last parties

Alice attended. "His typical flying visits. It's getting so difficult for our youngest daughter. She knows suitcases mean goodbyes. George believes Nixon's the best thing to hit America this century. He'll clean out the hippies and yippies for sure."

Trying to be friendly, Alice asked her what George thought of the Vietnam War. The woman never answered her question. Instead, she said, "But of course, you haven't been home for quite a while. How silly of me. Ah! there's Mr. Isaacs. Must say hello to him." As she moved away, she threw a final question at her. "Do you plan to return, umm?"

When left alone at parties, Alice was accustomed to the next eager male coming to ask her out, or the Managing Director's wife fixing her with an icy smile. Everybody seemed to know that she was a poor girl with little money to spend on dresses and probably no money to even think of returning home. Others thought of her as extremely stupid or excessively promiscuous. Alice suspected there were some who even resented her presence. But Vikram's family treated her as one of their own. They were fiercely protective about it.

Vikram often pleaded with her to accept some money. "But there must be things you want to buy for yourself," he'd say. Her answer was always the same. "Until Krishna comes home, just leave me enough money to pay for the meat and the vegetables. When the time comes, maybe you could buy me a passage home."

Vikram prided himself on not being an impulsive person. One day he suddenly came home with three beautiful *saris* and knew that his pride had been badly shaken. They were rich, heavy silks with fine designs woven in silver. He had spent hours in the shop. The salesmen knew both him and Krishna quite well. "Why don't you take these, sir?" one of them asked. "Your wife always loved these delicate pastel shades," he said, pointing to a shimmering heap of raw silk *saris*. Trying hard not to lose his patience, Vikram reminded him for the third time that evening, "These are not for my wife."

Alice quickly made beautiful dresses out of them. Then she felt she wanted something else, something for herself. It cost her a great deal of effort to ask Vikram for some money to buy shoes. So far, she had managed to get by on a small remittance she had received from her bank several months ago. But that had almost run out.

Vikram wouldn't hear of her apologies. He immediately arranged for a Chinese shoemaker to come to the house. When the shoes arrived a fortnight later, she was ecstatic. She wanted to try them on with her dresses, but was afraid she might offend somebody. Vikram wanted her to try them on too, but felt awkward about asking her. Malini's eager insistence made it easier for them both — for her to put them on, for him to ask her to.

Alice got dressed faster than anyone else Vikram could remember. Almost as soon as she had left them, Alice came and stood with the first of her dresses, blushing violently. Vikram described the dress to Malini as best he could. Alice returned to her room and came back this time in a slender ice-blue sheath which took his breath away. She returned one more time, looking lovelier. Malini continued to applaud her father's descriptions. What Vikram couldn't describe to her were the neat ankles, the narrow hips, the softly rounded belly, the faultless breasts, and a face that looked younger every moment. This colorful pageant stirred him uneasily. Vikram remembered the parties and wondered whether he hadn't unconsciously added fuel to the suspicions of others. His fellow Indians made no secret of their curiosity about her true relationship with him. The whites pretended they knew, and went contemptuously out of their way to humble her.

Of her new dresses, Alice wore only one to a party before she told Vikram, "I don't think I could stand another one of those disgusting cocktail parties. Whether I stay at home or behave naturally with you outside, they'll always think of me as your mistress." Vikram tried to smile away the anger rising in him.

"Your civilized friends don't approve of mistresses, real or imagined, publicly flaunted in their face. I don't think I want to go to another party." Alice smiled to make him feel better. "Besides, I enjoy staying home with Malini."

"Where is Malini?" asked Vikram.

"Fast asleep in my bed."

"Tell me you'll wear all those dresses at home," he said. "Only then will I stop inflicting the invitations on you." For the second time in his relationship with her, Vikram gave way to an impulse of the moment. He reached out and gathered her fingers in his hand.

Alice looked into his eyes. "You've been kind to me, Vikram," she said. "I've never known so much kindness in my life. It frightens me."

The silence, their nearness, all filled her with a strange foreboding. She was happy, and nervous because she was happy.

She had often tried to recall a lost mood from a picture taken by her father when she was four. It showed her standing beside a chicken coop with her hands on her hips. She believed it went to the heart of a mood born of the sheer exuberance of life on their small farm in Vermont. That was always her ideal. She hoped her present mood could move closer to the one lost in her childhood. She felt a sharp pang of remorse as she realized there was no turning back the hands of time.

Somewhere in the midst of her thoughts, Vikram was holding Alice in his arms. Then something happened, and they were fighting for their kisses like two crazy people. They fought until his lips smarted and her arms hurt from the cruel pressure of his fingers. Alice did not protest as he led her away to his bed where they clung to each other in the darkness. They were both afraid that their happiness, once forgotten, would never be the same again. And they were afraid to part.

"Will my scarred and broken body please you?" she asked.

"Yes, yes," he whispered breathlessly, as he dug his teeth into her shoulder. She winced with pain.

"Touch me," she begged. His impatient hands reeled and lurched across her burning body and stopped in sudden surprise over her hardening nipples. "Be gentle with me. For once be gentle with me," she cried.

As if in answer to her helpless moans, his hands moved away uncertainly. But his lips locked themselves on her breast and forced a stifled scream out of her. The next time their lips met, his hands slid down her back and found her buttocks heaving and delirious in a mounting frenzy matching his own.

She wanted him then. He was about to respond blindly.

Then something snapped within Vikram. He wilted in a flash, leaving her struggling and unquenched. As he came back to earth, he remembered her through a mist of pain. He didn't feel sorry for her any longer. No, he thought, this is not the road to Chirribilli. He was convinced she had set herself up for the beasts. His worst suspicions returned. He imagined her a dirty slut of a hitchhiker, spending nights in what she hoped would be exotic and mysterious arms. Perhaps trembling at the brutality. Maybe even despising the unexpected perversion. But always eager, always grateful for whatever little she could get out of the deal. Distraught and indignant, Vikram slipped out of her without any effort.

At first, she tried to cling to him desperately, floundering up the edge of fulfillment that dodged her senses. Then she realized it had eluded her grasp, and sat up wondering what happened. She stared into the dark and asked, "Is something the matter?"

He wanted to tell her then that he found her cloying softness unendurable. His lust had become brittle and insensitive from the scorching passion of her secret recesses. He cursed himself for his folly. He wanted to hurt her. The real concern that she felt as she waited for the sound of his voice, her pain at what she imagined to be their mutual disappointment, these meant nothing to him. Vikram was furious with himself for having been led so far. Even more furious to find his unconquered desire still urging him on. "I'm feeling sick," he said.

She threw her arms over his neck and leaned over his shoulder. As their bodies touched once again, Vikram felt a renewed surge of shame and disgust sweeping over him. He pushed her away roughly. "Don't," he hissed, "it's you who's making me sick."

Alice fumbled until she switched on the lamp. "What's the matter with you, Vikram?" she asked.

"Go away. Go away," he cried.

Alice could not believe she was awake. "What have I done wrong?" she begged. "You ached for love just as much as I did, did you not?"

He waved her off. "Go away," he cried angrily. "Don't torment me. I feel sullied. I feel terribly dirty."

Alice knew then that it was not her defeat. Her voice was slow and bitter. "Sullied by my body, no doubt," she said. Her tearful laugh was hollow and mocking. "After Chirribilli my body will never be the same, will it? Or Krishna's, for that matter. Or Malini's. At first, I couldn't understand why you were so distant to us, how you could be so cold, uncaring, and aloof. I told myself I was reading you all wrong. Your pain touched me, Vikram, or what I mistook to be pain. That's why I stayed on. But it wasn't that, was it? I can almost see you, cringing in a corner of your mind, more disgusted than concerned, more repelled than sorrowful. Every time you spoke to us, looked at us, you sullied yourself just that much more. Some of our dirt rubbed off on you. It's a wonder how I got as far as I did. A great wonder. That was the biggest mistake of all. Yours and mine. Oh Vikram! it caught up with me even as I was gasping to give you what so many have wrenched out of me." Alice cried as she spoke. But Vikram remained seething and unmoved.

She recovered quickly. Her voice was soft and controlled when she spoke again. "It was not torn out of me along the tea gardens up north," she said. "It would've been better there. In the moist, yielding earth. But they chose the Cooch Behar Passenger train for me, a third class compartment reeking of excrement and ripe mangoes. They spoke a language I did not understand, a language whose nuances and inflexions I found intriguing. One of them waved me away from the open door where I stood and watched your great countryside flashing by. Then I saw they looked sullen and angry. Was it the sense of freedom I felt that was so hateful to them? I wondered. Then one of the men stood up and began to bolt both the doors. They were upon me one after the other. Seventeen men. Maybe more. They were very determined men. They even seemed disciplined in a strange kind of way. They were patient and knew what a woman had to offer. I seem to remember only their eyes now. Big white eyes straining out of their sockets, and little red veins and specks like star dust. Then I remember the silent road, the truck, and you. It's funny. I'm beginning to cry again," she said, wiping away her tears.

As she stood up from the bed and straightened her crumpled dress, Alice smiled warmly at Vikram. "I hate to ask," she said, "but could you please arrange that passage to Boston?"

Eleven

BUT ALICE stayed on. Not because of Vikram, for it was Krishna who suddenly appeared like a ghost one morning. It was her father who brought her home, cradling Krishna like a baby in his powerful arms. It looked like the stuff of myths to those who caught even a fleeting glimpse of the bearded man with a trident in one hand and a woman clasped in the other, riding in an open Jeep. When they reached the house in the early hours of the morning, everyone believed God had unleashed a rare miracle and brought back a spirit from the dead. The servants fell to the ground at Sambhu Narain's feet. Even Vikram trembled before he had so much as touched Krishna for fear he would find her ethereal, the substance of dreams.

For Alice, it was as if characters in a legend were walking out of the pages of a book. She held a frightened Malini, suddenly awakened in the middle of the night. Alice whispered into her ears that her mother was back. She came close to Krishna and Malini instinctively reached out and clung to her, crying, "Mama! Mama! you've come back to us."

There was a flicker of a smile on Krishna's lips as she returned Malini's embrace. She seemed more composed than excited over the reunion, for not a word escaped her. She sat silently as her in-laws soon came over and wept and sobbed over her.

Krishna looked pale, weak, and bloodied. Sir Ajoy asked Sambhu Narain if she shouldn't be taken to a hospital right away. He looked with infinte tenderness at Krishna for a long time and finally nodded his head. Vikram and his parents drove her to a nursing home within a matter of minutes.

Alice seemed unable to control herself any longer. She too wept like a child with the others.

By next morning, Sambhu Narain was gone, having offered nothing to anyone by way of an explanation for Krishna's return. His driver waited with the Jeep for a full day until Janaki Devi came down from Bishnupur and asked the driver to return. The only detail the driver could offer was that he had driven from Benapole on the Bangladesh border. Krishna's mother said we were unlikely to see her husband again for a long time, if ever. Then she too left for her village, saying, "I know my poor girl is now in good hands."

After the first wave of joy and excitement died down, Vikram's house drifted into a curious state of apathy. Alice was the one person whose excitement knew no bounds. She spent all her time with Malini. Malini was the reason, she said, why Krishna had come back, and no one seemed to doubt her word. Vikram avoided her, and ended up avoiding Malini in the process. Alice could see what was happening, and hoped Krishna would come home soon.

She often wanted to visit her in the nursing home. Somehow, things couldn't be arranged for her to go before visiting hour was over. It was also strange that Vikram seldom volunteered any information about Krishna to his parents or anyone else. When asked, he would simply say she was better. Alice thought perhaps he didn't want Malini to go visit her mother and was therefore discouraging others from going as well. After a while, even Malini stopped asking about her mother. The walls of silence grew higher around the house each day. Conversation was too much of an effort. Words, when they floated through the air on rare occasions, sounded stupid and purposeless.

Alice couldn't believe she hadn't exchanged a single word with Krishna from the time they had met. She was intrigued by her and wanted to know more about her, her life with Vikram. She longed for the rare thrill that follows an unexpected insight gained into the lives of others. Alice wondered, as she wondered over others, if she would ever discover what small insignificant events took place in the private borders of Vikram and Krishna's lives. What they said to each other when no one was around, how they loved one another. In a way, she seemed to know it all. But that was not enough.

After Vikram left for work one morning, Malini ran into her room. "Do you know, Alice?" she cried excitedly. "Mama's coming home today." Alice was just as excited as Malini and asked if her father had given her the news. "No, don't be silly," she replied, "I heard him mention it to the cook."

It wouldn't be the last time Alice would experience such a sudden surge of disappointment.

Krishna returned to a house accustomed to silence. Her added presence made not the slightest difference to the place. If anything, it grew more inhibited and tended to discourage visitors. Would be sympathizers felt uneasy over the apparent futility of their visits. Even the servants grew more remote, from their masters as well as among themselves. Very diffidently, the cook asked Krishna one day if she would like to order the weekly shopping like she used to before. Without raising her eyes from the album of family photographs she was trying to hide behind some books, she asked him in a bland, expressionless voice what he had been doing all the while she was away. When the cook admitted Vikram had left the shopping entirely to him, she said, "Do as you've been doing."

She disliked being asked any questions, even by Malini. "Mama, do you like the way Alice has done my hair?" she asked one day.

"What does Alice think of it?" Krishna said simply. When told of Alice's opinion that it suited her perfectly, Krishna said, "Then it must be nice," before returning to a magazine she was reading.

It was a bleak house, its bleakness relieved only by Malini's footsteps as she rushed in and out of the ever-waiting arms of Alice. Her laughter was like a breath of fresh air in an otherwise musty room. Alice skillfully drew out her laughter, and it echoed through the entire house. She loved the story of the magic pudding most of all. "More, more," she cried, as she clapped her hands in delight. But Alice was careful to drag on the story from one day to another. It gave them both something to look forward to.

It was a strange house where people spoke in single syllables and barely nodded in answer. There was no room for idle talk, no dialogue where ideas are picked up, accepted, or rejected. Only Malini weaved in and out of people's separate worlds. But she too was losing her taste for Krishna's passionless kisses, Vikram's cold embraces, and his flat, tired voice. Krishna didn't seem to mind Malini spending most of her time with Alice. Alice began to suspect it really didn't make any difference to her.

Alice's presence in the house had come to be an accepted fact. She realized of course she was only fulfilling Malini's needs, needs a well-trained nanny could probably meet just as well. But she seemed quite content to play the role, careful not to overstep its limits. She felt neither passion nor pity for Vikram. But in the back of her mind there lurked the hope that Rahul would show up before long. Nobody seemed to know where he was. He wasn't in his village home, that much was certain from the letters Janaki Devi sent from time to time.

Krishna was beginning to turn cold without being cruel, inconsiderate without being offensive, indifferent without even trying. At the same time, Vikram's life became mired in self-pity. Malini's contented prattle, as she spoke to herself or laughed with Alice, couldn't shake them out of their apathy.

Malini began to avoid the rest of the house. In the midst of her ramblings, she would stop and come into Alice's room. She came for no apparent reason. She just liked being there. Alice would look up from her bed or her desk and put aside whatever she was doing at the sound of the doorknob clicking softly. She waited for the crack in the door to widen slowly, as Malini tried to follow the sounds and fix her presence. A moment's pause, and then she would rush to the bed, delighted at what she always imagined to be a complete surprise for Alice. Alice sang to her, taught her poems, or simply lay in bed with her, fingers playing with her curls as she stared into her blighted eyes.

While she was lying in Alice's bed one day, Malini suddenly asked, "Why doesn't Granpa come visit us more often? When he brought Mama home the other night, do you know what he said? He held me tight and said there was a special place in his heart for me. Wonder what he meant?"

Alice explained he meant everyone loved Malini, but that her Granpa from the village loved her most of all. As Malini thought over this, Alice found her thoughts drifting to Rahul. She was beginning to lose heart over seeing him again.

"Mama is not well today," confided Jyoti on a particularly sultry afternoon. "She is very silent." As usual, Malini had asked her how she liked her hair that particular day, and was expecting the usual reply that it was very nice. On this day, Krishna didn't even say that.

The days became interminably long for everyone. Krishna spent her days walking in the garden or walking through the house as she adjusted a vase here or wiped a speck of dust somewhere. Sometimes she moved an ashtray from one room to the other or opened windows and shut them again. The few hopeful guests and faithful friends who still persisted in coming to the house went back in despair.

Vikram hardly spoke to Alice, but he asked Krishna the same questions each night and received the same answers. If he found her staring at the ceiling, he would ask, "Aren't you going to sleep, Krishna?" She would say, yes, and simply close her eyes.

Even the most trifling gestures of married people ceased between them. He got into bed from the south, she from the north. Next morning, they left the same way. She for her breakfast and endless walks through the house, he for his breakfast and office.

On certain days, Krishna asked Alice if she had slept well the night before, and not say another word to her for the rest of the day. Vikram also told Malini from time to time to be nice to Alice, but he would rarely lift his eyes off the morning papers when speaking.

Today, Vikram said the same thing, but added that it would be a special day because Janaki Devi was coming from Bishnupur. With her mouth overflowing with buttered toast, Malini asked if Granpa was coming too. She looked sad to hear he was not.

Although Janaki Devi had visited Krishna twice in the nursing home, each time she had stayed with Lady Ranu. Alice had never had a chance to see her. When Vikram brought his mother-in-law home late that afternoon, Alice was fascinated by her. Krishna introduced her to the frail woman in white. "This is my mother," she said, with an unusual outpouring of warmth. "Isn't she nice?"

Alice held her hand and said she looked truly wonderful. Krishna smiled sadly and buried her face in her mother's arms. When she looked up and turned around moments later, her face was quite expressionless.

Vikram couldn't understand why she didn't cry and get it over with. He felt an awful burden of guilt and wished she would cry so he could go down on his knees and beg forgiveness, as much for himself as for others. He grew more desperate the more he saw Krishna and her mother move closer to one another. An exquisite feeling of hatred now began to grow within him. It was starting to poison his thoughts and relationships even at work. But the feeling was really directed mostly at himself. He had forgotten how to love Krishna. But he did want to love her all over again and prayed she wouldn't damn him with her indifference. In her presence, he now began to feel unwashed. He began to feel the same way in Malini's presence too. One day, watching Malini learning a poem from Alice, he found himself choking for want of air. He rushed outside the house and steadied himself against the railing of the verandah. Something held his heart in a vice of steel. This was it, he thought. But it was only a wave of nausea. It soon passed.

Could it be that Malini's life was wasting away? There were no schools Vikram would care to send her to where she might learn. At least she was learning something from Alice. He knew he would soon have to take a good hard look at immigration, if only to take care of Malini's education. The city, his country for that matter, had nothing to offer him.

Alice would've liked to know Janaki Devi better, but she

never knew what to talk to her about. The subject of Rahul was, of course, closest to Alice's heart, but she also knew it would be terribly indiscreet to broach it. She wondered why Janaki Devi insisted on wearing white when she was not a widow, and it remained a mystery to her because she couldn't find anyone to discuss Sambhu Narain with either. When Janaki Devi prepared to return to Bishnupur after several weeks, Vikram casually asked her in front of Alice how Rahul was doing. He had come home at last, then disappeared again, and that was when Alice found out he was perhaps within her reach.

When Malini crept into her room that night, she asked Alice what she was doing. "I'm trying to think what to write to my mother," she said. In an earlier incarnation, she might have written she had a job looking after a little blind girl, that her parents were so rich they had servants even to wash the dishes. Now it sounded so trivial. She had hardly seen the city, so what could she tell them about it? Perhaps only that when the Queen was here recently, the streets were sprayed with perfume. Yes, people were stranger than she had seen anywhere else. The look in some of their eyes made you think they were plotting to overthrow the government, when they're probably debating whether to buy fish or mutton that day. Alice was getting wiser by the day.

"So what will you write your mother?" asked Malini.

"I'm going to tell her I love being with Malini. I couldn't be happier."

Twelve

LADY RANU suddenly increased her visits to Vikram's house Her otherwise forlorn and martyred mood underwent a remarkable change. People actually saw her smile. There was even an air of suppressed excitement in her walk. All this could mean one of many things. Mostly, it suggested total involvement in some cause or the other. Whenever she sensed a critical situation — and her senses in this regard were extremely sharp — she would throw herself in its midst, but only if she cared.

Be it summer or winter, she would arrive heaving, perspiring, and out of breath. Thereafter, she would immediately assume full responsibility for all the important details. Brushing aside all suggestions, she would apply herself to her, or somebody else's, mission with undivided zeal. Although she effectively plugged up all other sources of cooperation around her, people found her presence rather comforting. Whether it was to organize a wedding or a funeral, or take care of a sick child or mother, she was always willing, always welcome. But only as long as she cared, for she was apt to lose interest in her projects, as she liked to call them, as quickly as she rushed into them.

Yes, it had been a long time since anyone saw Lady Ranu smile. Today, even her eyes were smiling. Looking resplendent in an orange Mysore silk *sari*, she appeared quite mysterious over the matter of taking Krishna out in the morning. She refused Vikram's car and expressed a preference for a common cab. On her way back home, she even talked Krishna into visiting her hair-dresser. By the time Vikram returned home that evening, she had just about driven everyone crazy with her secret excitement.

"Are you not feeling well, mother?" asked Vikram, noticing an unfamiliar expression on her face. He tried to introduce a note of humor in his voice, for his mother's obvious happiness had touched him too.

Lady Ranu pretended she hadn't heard him, and tried for a few more moments to appear as casual and unconcerned as she could. But then her arms flew up in the air, and there were tears of joy in her eyes. Her voice quivered with emotion as she announced that Dr. Mitra, the family gynecologist, had confirmed that very morning that Krishna was expecting once more.

Vikram looked blankly at his mother. It seemed she had spoken in a language he did not understand. It's impossible to know what thoughts rushed through his mind at that moment, but it is true he kept staring foolishly from his mother to Krishna for what must have been a long time. He had no illusions about what other men might have done to her, but it seemed cruel now to harbor dark suspicions on this seemingly happy occasion, to set himself apart from the others.

Krishna looked down at the cup of tea in front of her, the color rising in her cheeks. Vikram saw this and found no trouble convincing himself that it was his child she was carrying and no one else's. Still, something held him back even from rising up and touching her hand, let alone throw his arms around her. In the presence of others, the possibility of a kiss didn't even cross his mind.

From the moment she heard the news, Alice was dying to share her delight with Krishna. It was a long time before she found her alone in her room. She walked over to Krishna shyly. "I'm so happy for you," she said. As Alice reached out and touched her cheek, Krishna looked back into her eyes. In that exchange, each divined some hidden message of hope and fulfillment in the other, and they both felt glad.

Alice told Malini the next morning she might soon have a baby brother to play with, since she had been so good.

"Where is he now?" asked Malini excitedly.

"He's inside your mother," explained Alice, "like you were long ago."

"Where?" Malini asked again, and Alice had to show her by taking her hand and placing it against her tummy. Later that afternoon, Malini got up from Alice's bed and silently walked into Krishna's room. She walked up to the bed and placed her hands against Krishna's body. "Mama, my baby brother is here, isn't he?"

"Yes, Malini," replied Krishna, laughing till it brought tears to her eyes. Malini threw her arms around her waist and kissed her baby brother inside over and over again. When Alice looked into the room an hour later, she found Malini and Krishna fast asleep in each other's arms. She found it difficult to move away from the door. There was a sense of wonder in her heart and a great heaviness in her feet.

If not the baby, Malini's imagination and exuberance certainly drew the family a little closer. One day, she was sitting with her face resting on one hand, looking very thoughtful and troubled. Krishna asked her, "Whatever's the matter with you today?"

"Mama," she said, "I'd like my baby brother to sit beside me at table. I wonder if Alice will be able to feed us both. Can she?"

Vikram rarely looked up from his reading, but this time he did. "I think your mother'll have to feed your brother at least for some time," he said, "or Alice'll never get through her own meals." Vikram caught everyone by surprise coming out of his impenetrable shell of self-pity.

"Oh well!" sighed Malini with an air of resignation that would have been more apt for an adult. "But he can sit with me afterwards, can't he?" For the privilege of having him sit with her, she seemed quite willing to promise Krishna that she would play with her brother all day. Her imagination ran wild with the anticipated role of her brother's protector. She told Krishna what she thought of the woolies she was knitting, whether or not they felt suitably soft against the skin. She recommended vast quantities of socks and caps as a defense against mosquitoes. She was pleased with the idea of her old crib being hauled out of storage, happy and pensive as she stroked the wooden frame with her hand. But she cried out in pain as a tiny splinter of wood suddenly pierced her skin. She howled while Alice pried it out with a needle. Later, she explained the tears were not all for her. She was more concerned about what horrible disasters might befall her brother in that crib.

Next day, Vikram was compelled to call in the furniture painters. They had an impossible time trying to meet Malini's exacting standards for sanding and enamel paints. Lucky for them the last coat hadn't dried when it was time to go, or Malini might well have re-examined the surface and demanded another coat of paint.

She spent hours arranging and separating her toys. Finally, she informed Alice one day she had made up her mind about which toys she would leave entirely to her brother. Since she didn't want everyone to be throwing them around, would Alice please lock them up in the closet? And maybe she could ask her mother to make some new dresses for her favorite dolls.

Krishna had in fact been making dresses, cutting up material, sewing and stitching at a furious pace. But these were not for dolls. Malini was constantly asking her the colors of the dresses she was stitching on any particular day. She would lie for hours in Krishna's bed, holding her face in her hands, lost in thought, asking worrisome questions forming in her mind. Was that dress going to have a bunny rabbit on it? Was Krishna going to put any soft frills on this one?

Somehow, Krishna and, it seemed, just about everyone else around her knew the baby was a boy. Magic! "But darling," Krishna tried to explain, "boys don't like frills on their clothes."

Even after she had been persuaded to examine Vikram's clothes, Malini was far from happy with the idea of no frills. In fact, she had great hopes her brother might eventually wear some of her old clothes which she knew to be preserved in mothballs. She was unhappy, and a little disturbed, as she came face to face with inexplicable differences between boys' and girls' clothes. She drew some comfort when told she could dress her brother in the evenings if she wanted to.

Very soon, the *sari* proved a poor disguise for Krishna's pregnancy. So Alice stitched her a few dresses. Krishna found them so comfortable she kept adding to their numbers each week. "I'll give these all to you after I've finished with them," she told Alice. They both found it very amusing.

Alice remembered how Herman very nearly got her into those damned dresses. Vermont seemed such a perfect place to meet that towering blond-haired stud from Brown in Rhode Island. He chased her across the snow, his deep voice calling out her name. She was angry at his presumptuousness as she sped down the slopes and swung round to face him at the bottom of the run. He bowed and presented her with the notebook she had lost the previous day. For once, she had wished winter would never end. On their second visit to the Lodge a month or so later, she told him she might be expecting. She meant it as a joke, but he was devastated. Herman cowered on his knees and wept in her lap. Oh! what had he done to her, he cried between his stifled sobs. He was not a student after all, as he had led her to believe, but a rising star in the Brown faculty. His wife was wintering with her parents in St. Croix. She would never agree to a divorce, and he could never give up his tenure at Brown.

But oh! How he loved Alice.

An Australian room-mate had a cautionary message for her: Never shack up with a man until you've checked out his number. Married men'll jigger you up and then say how sorry they are. She loved the word, jigger. Alice told Herman not to worry. She'd find a way out of the sticky wicket, another one of her friend's priceless Australian expressions. Alice decided she'd tell Krishna the story some other time. Tell her also how much she loved the *sari*. It seemed a beautiful *sari* always weaves an illusion. The *sari* lasts for years and years and one never grows old in it. She remembered someone telling her, "Twenty years from now, you'll still look the same in it, ageless as the *sari*."

I had been visiting Vikram's house from time to time. A week before Krishna was due to go in for her baby, I phoned the house. She received the call and pretended she was angry. Told me she was offended I had called instead of coming over right away. Unannounced, as always. I knew too well that it would never again be like always, like the times when her brother Rahul was around. But when I heard Krishna's voice on the phone, I felt a bit stupid to think of those things.

I hadn't seen her for weeks. Her features were perhaps a little without depth, a little thickened, but Krishna's beauty remained undimmed. In Vikram's living room, it was once again like always, or so it seemed. Even Malini surprised me, kissing me with an innocent passion I could not understand. She laughed in embarrassment as the kiss missed its mark and came to rest on my nose. The next time, she kissed me hard on the lips, and I held her in my hands, eager to touch her skin, to breathe her innocence, to forget my own sense of mortality. We talked about Ravi Shankar and the magic he had created with Menuhin. I mentioned a British Council fellowship I had been promised, and was forced to start a long list of things to bring back from Europe. A length of chiffon from Paris for Krishna, Swiss chocolates for Malini, a new Ronson lighter for Vikram. Would Alice like something for herself, I asked, seeing her sitting in our midst. I caught her blushing. "Nothing really," she said, "I think I have everything I need."

The servants beamed with pleasure as Vikram ordered sherry for the ladies and scotch and soda for the men. Alice looked surprised. She had no idea these things existed in her surroundings. For the first time since she came to the house, Vikram put on some music on the stereo. The strains of sitar music created just the right mood as we ate kebabs and fried prawns and noted how poor the servants were when compared to Hamid. Like other servants before him, Hamid too was fading from their memory.

Of course, we talked politics. How could we not, being Bengalis? "Look at their party emblem," exclaimed Vikram. "Twin bulls, if you please. It's this underlying sexuality that'll undo the Congress party."

Now there were some really good days ahead of them all. If Vikram had any misgivings about the child, he had laid them to rest. Alice thought she could see a real tenderness and concern in his new relationship with Krishna. The house had come back to life.

There was a time, a long time ago, when the place was full of sounds. When they disappeared, one couldn't even hear rubber slippers and their padded footfalls on the carpet. Nor the watchman's wooden sandals startling the night as he walked up and down the concrete driveway on his rounds. Alice had wondered if no one moved chairs in that house, or opened cupboards, or break china. Even the sound of pots and pans being scrubbed had gone. Now they were back. A spell had been lifted.

If she felt any fear, Krishna didn't show it. She was obsessed with her child and her quickening expectation swept along everyone around her. Everyone hoped that this awakening would somehow wash away the tragedies that floated so perilously close to Krishna's life. She told Alice how she thought things might be turning around. She was feeling better after a long, long time.

Perhaps even Malini would find her sight someday. It suddenly became unthinkable to her that her daughter wouldn't share in all its fullness the joy the unborn child promised.

It was time for Krishna to go in for the baby. Once in the nursing home, however, she kept on waiting and waiting. Vikram dropped in every evening, so did Malini and Alice. Janaki Devi wrote to say she would visit the child after Krishna came home, but Lady Ranu was more than happy to play the role of her mother.

When no one was around, Krishna liked to pull up a chair next to the window. The view from her window was singularly unattractive, but it held a strange fascination for her. She could see part of an enormous concrete building with what looked like little balconies glued to them wherever possible. Then there were the weather-stained tiles, red long ago, sloping down the roof of a building she could not see. There were also some twisted branches of a scrawny *gul mohur* tree. Only the color of the tiles changed with the light. Dull on a cloudy day, a little brighter after a shower, orange in the hot sun reflected off the whitewashed walls nearby. One day, she saw a few extra leaves on the lowest branch of the *gul mohur* tree. The next day saw a fresh twig of flowers in bloom. One night a storm struck down a dead branch and left behind an ugly, jagged scar.

Fluttering from the balconies, there were *saris* stretched out to dry — purple, crimson, green, lemon. The next day, the colors changed. On some days, there was no washing in some of the apartments. Old colors appeared every so often, spread over railings one remembered. Unexpected patterns and objects erupted in spaces where nothing was seen for days. A cotton dress with large, dark circles, a pair of jeans airing in the sun. Young servant girls and fat-armed matrons made occasional appearances. Men in cotton vests and pajamas often stared blankly at the hospital windows. Towards evening, or earlier if it rained, the *saris* would be plucked out of the air one by one. White and black bras and men's underwear moved fast from the innermost lines of washing. They were always kept away from direct exposure to the road, away from the prurient eyes of rascals who might imagine buttocks, breasts, and who knew what else snug or ripening behind the drying underwear. When it was dark, there was no more color, only geometric shapes of light — sickly in places, bright, flickering, and fluorescent elsewhere. Dark silhouettes pursued nameless chores behind the open doors and windows.

There came a time when Krishna could only imagine these changing shapes and colors, when she could no longer leave the bed and walk over to the kaleidoscope framed in her window. Now she waited for her hour and bit her lips every time a wave of pain shot through her body. For two nights, she strained and groaned in vain. When the doctors finally knew she couldn't endure any more, they cut her open.

In the first few moments of shock, Vikram wished he could throw up in the polished, white-tiled corridors. What an infinite waste of pain. The heaving, screaming contortions of birth suddenly seemed senseless, utterly meaningless. It was not unusual in the city, he thought, to see a man, walking barefoot down the street holding in his arms some object wrapped in white linen. As the man walked, one end of the bundle bobbed loosely up and down. But not so the other end, and one knew right away which side was the head. Then it wasn't too difficult to imagine the little body inside. Vikram thought it strange that a man should cradle a dead child in his arms exactly as women hold them living. Surely there must be other ways to carry a parcel destined for cremation. His own image walking barefoot with an inert form swaddled in his arms nearly drove him out of his mind. It followed him into his home as he brushed past Alice waiting eagerly for news, followed him all the way to his drugged sleep.

Nobody asked Alice to go to the nursing home. But she wasn't sure who would be around to comfort Krishna when she woke up from her sedation. Krishna seemed to recognize her. She smiled in her euphoria as Alice dabbed away the beads of perspiration on her face. There was no need to comfort Krishna, not just yet. At night Alice whispered to Malini, "It'll be a little while longer before your baby brother comes home." Malini sensed her sadness and started to cry.

thirteen

IF MALINI was missing anything in her life there was no way of knowing. She never complained that she mght be getting left behind by experiences common to most children. One probably needs to get older to experience such abstractions as feeling empty inside.

But hers was a narrow, constricted world where she did not know the love of friends, only that of parents and grandparents. Alice's affection was something new to her. But no aunts or cousins ever pampered her. Her nearness held a deep sense of fear for most relatives. It was as if she mirrored and held up before them one of the many terrors of conception. She was a warning to people who thought of themselves as normal, well-adjusted human beings, a warning to aspiring patriarchs of the profound bitterness forever casting its shadow on the transmission of life. The aunts and uncles did in fact convey their concern for Malini and Krishna, but they chose to do so over the telephone or through accidental meetings, rather than planned visits to the house in Ballygunge, a monumental testimony to their deepest fears.

She lived for sounds, and they in turn helped shape her world. Once more, the house became oddly stifling. The sounds Malini loved began to elude her. Even the sounds she heard no longer interested her. There was no doubt summer had a hand in this, for summer spread its damnation on all things, scorching everything a little more, killing everything a little more. Summer was silent. Malini had trouble getting used to a sense of summer. She was learning to dread the silence of the house.

"Why is Mama coming home alone?" she finally asked one day, her voice choking with tears. "Where is my baby brother?"

Vikram turned and walked away without answering her. Alice stood there in silence until she couldn't stand the hurt in Malini's face any longer. She drew her close to herself and said, "I'm sorry your brother is dead, Malini. You'll never see him again." Having said this, she felt as shocked and stunned as Malini. They clung to each other and cried for a long time. Malini didn't remember her uncle Sanjit, but she sobbed and asked about Rani, her sometime friend from the house across the road. Rani was gone too, for months now. Shutting her mind to whatever pain the word evoked, she closed her eyes and asked if Rani too was dead. Wasn't she? She found it hard to accept the sudden void that opened up before her, just as she took a long time to understand that Rani would never again come to play with her toys, or Hamid take her for walks through the garden. It was like a guest calling up on the evening of the party to say he wouldn't come, and the most important guest at that.

Malini searched for signs and confirmations, inwardly hoping for the impossible. When she found one day that the baby's cot had been quietly removed from Krishna's room, she asked Alice to bring out the toys she had put aside for her brother. There was no point setting them aside.

In spite of the occasional showers, it was turning out to be another bad summer for the city. Water trucks struggled in and out of slums and other parts of the city so people might have something to drink. Most of the taps were running dry, the old tube wells gave out more clanking, rattling sounds than water. When they did spit out a few drops, it met the needs of only a handful. Newspapers pounced on the city councilors for their neglect. They in turn pointed to the suppliers who had stacked the water-works yards with sub-standard coal which caused the huge pumps to break down. Everyone forgot about the men who had actually graded and certified the coal on behalf of the water-works. Forgotten were the men, women, and children who rushed out of their homes with saucepans, buckets, and kerosene cans the moment a water truck entered their area. They ran with the truck until it stopped. In the mad scramble, men tripped over women, women pushed aside children, and children fought each other for spots in the queue.

Vikram worked his way through much of this everyday drama of life on his way to the nursing home. He parked his car and lit a cigarette, remembering a time when he and Krishna forgot what it was to talk to each other, to touch each other. He thought he had helped change it by thinking unwaveringly of the child. There was something to look forward to, something to prepare for, and the words came back without prompting.

His attention was drawn to a first floor window on the opposite side of the quadrangle. A woman's figure, clad in a loose, printed dress which accentuated her distended belly, kept appearing and reappearing in the window. She was pacing restlessly through the room, pausing briefly to look outside as she passed the window. She reminded Vikram of a caged animal facing the world with fury, turning away from the bars in bursts of hopelessness. He found himself picturing her in the act of love, prolonging the drama to its last breath and wondering perversely how she might react to the birth of a deformed child or a dead child. He swore at her and wished her the worst. Instantly, he was overcome with shame. Perhaps he would tell Krishna she could have another baby. The truth was he didn't know how to go about picking up the broken pieces of their shattered dreams and putting them together again.

Krishna thanked the nurses who helped her into the car. She barely recognized Vikram. Neither could he find anything to say to her as he drove home. He thought of trying to console her, comfort her, to draw her attention to inconsequential things. Nothing would work, he knew that for certain. He even thought of quoting from the beatitudes he found so deeply moving as a child. The priests who had taught him that, and many other things, would surely have approved. His first boss, a bald-headed New Zealander, would probably have asked him to give her a stiff shot of brandy. Can't let little things crush your spirit, he was fond of saying. The engine must keep turning.

The crowds and the traffic stretched out the journey home

to what seemed like an age. He swore under his breath, but was afraid to so much as brush against a pedestrian. His car marked him as privileged, vulnerable to violence.

Krishna crouched forward as she leaned and stepped out of the car. Perhaps it was the pain in her wound that hadn't completely healed. Whatever it was, there was something peculiar about the way she walked, with her wrists crossed in front of her, arms slightly drawn, shoulders hunched. She walked very slowly and went straight into her room and to her bed. There she sat down with her legs crossed. Her eyes moved to Alice who had followed her into the room. Very softly, she said, "Please draw the curtains." When Alice had done that, she said, 'Now shut the doors, please.' As Alice moved towards the door, she saw Malini standing outside, looking sad and miserable. Alice brought her in and guided her to the bed. Vikram walked in behind them.

"Mama, Mama," Malini cried, as she touched Krishna's arm. "You've come back at last. Promise me you won't go away again."

"Go away, go away," cried Krishna in a hard, rasping voice, adding, "Not now." Vikram was standing behind Krishna at the head of the bed. He reached out and drew Malini to himself. She looked contrite and ashamed, like she had spoken out of turn in the company of adults.

"Have you shut the door?" asked Krishna. The question was addressed to no one in particular.

Alice had forgotten. Now, as she pulled the door shut, the room suddenly became almost totally dark.

"Switch on the lights, please," said Krishna. "No, not those," she said quickly as Alice moved towards a panel of switches next to the door. "Only the ones beside the bed."

Arms drawn, shoulders bent, she rested her hands in her lap, palms facing up and wrists crossed. She sat in that posture of motherhood for some time. She looked round once, then lifted a hand and undid the clasps of her blouse. Vikram closed his eyes as the light bounced off the smooth and terrible scars where Krishna's breasts had been sliced off. Alice stared in horror and fascination.

A smile played on Krishna's lips. She hummed a familiar ditty, one that mothers in Bengal have hummed or sung for ages. With rapt attention, she went through the motions of holding the baby's head steady with one hand and inserting the nipple into the mouth with the other. Then she gently rocked herself from side to side and continued to hum her song.

They stood in the shadows. With the doors shut, the heavy curtains sealed off the room from all other sound. Alice was transfixed by the scars, a light shade of brown marring the even paleness of her complexion. Vikram stood with tears in his eyes. Malini held on to his hand tightly, but her mother's singing brought a glow of unexpected happiness to her face. Krishna stopped her humming and looked up at the shadows. Her eyes moved, vaguely searching for something. Her silent audience didn't seem to bother her. She resumed her humming, but stopped just as abruptly.

"Alice," she said.

"Yes?"

"Please leave the purple dress for me."

"Of course, Krishna. They're all yours." There was sorrow

and tenderness in her voice.

Krishna fastened the clasps of her blouse and gathered the *sari* around herself. With her imaginary newborn on her shoulder, she started pacing the room. She patted it to sleep with a slow rhythm, ever so gently as mothers have done for a thousand years and more.

"Doesn't a jacaranda tree flower in winter?" she asked, once again addressing the question to no one in particular. "In January when the oranges are ripe? .... What will it be, a grave or a pyre? .... Such a sweet little baby brother....

"Please take my *saris* instead, I haven't finished with the dresses yet.... Will you please, Alice?"

"Yes, Krishna," replied Alice, the tears flowing freely down her cheeks.

Then Krishna turned to her husband. "It should be fun visiting the gardens, Vikram.... Whatever happened to Roger Ames? .... Shhh! not now, my dear. No, no, no, don't you see she's blind? .... Are there poppies in the garden?

"Go bring me some, Vikram, please."

"There are none, Krishna," he said in a broken voice.

Krishna laughed. "Does it matter? .... Oh Alice! you can't have the gold brocade *sari*, my wedding *sari*....

"Butter and tons of sandalwood for my dear father. I want to wear that gold *sari* again for him.... Please leave the flowers there. There, at the foot of the crucifix.... See, Vikram, just see how big his eyes are. I look so huge in those dresses."

Krishna paused and looked longingly down her shoulder. "You can go now," she whispered, turning to Vikram and then to Alice. "See, see, he's fast asleep."

fourteen

KIRPAL SINGH tracked Vikram down to his home. Said he had always wanted to find out what happened to his little girl. When he saw Malini he couldn't believe it was the same person he remembered as a broken doll in the field. He was even more astonished to find Alice in the same house. He was naturally curious, but saved his curiosity for another time.

Alice was no less surprised to see Kirpal Singh. "I never really thanked you for all you did for us," she said.

Kirpal had changed from his earlier image of a *kurta* and *churidar*-clad truck driver. In his new suit, a red silk tie, and a freshly starched turban, he could well pass for a film star or a maharajah. He explained that he was in town for an interview at the U.S. consulate. His number had come up, he was going to emigrate to the States. With a hearty laugh that shook his enormous body, he assured Alice she would have plenty of opportunities to thank him once he was there. He wasn't sure where, but it could be New York or New Jersey.

Turning to Vikram, he said he had had it with India. It was getting from bad to worse in North Bengal, his normal business route, and he wished the young men there all the luck. "I've made my peace with them, those young firebrands," he said. "When I last drove past the gardens a few months ago, young students stopped my truck dozens of times and demanded I say *Lal Salam*. I always obliged them. So what? I lose nothing in giving the red salute. Some of them even cornered me one day with bows and arrows and spears. They wanted me to go down on my knees and garland a large photograph of Chairman Mao. What should I have done? Wait for the police? The poor beggars didn't dare leave the police station for fear it might be taken over by Naxalites. These days they can't seem to move without marching in division strength. Do you know what happened to Amarjit Brar, a Sikh manager in Dimog Estate? They beat him up with iron rods near Mal, then buried him in the soil with his neck and head sticking out of a pile of stones. By the time the police came, ants had carved out a passage through his cheeks. When they pushed away the stones, the ants came running through holes that once held his eyes. So what did I do? I garlanded Mao. I didn't think I was running away from a fight. There's nothing to run away from. There's nowhere one can run to."

Kirpal Singh talked Vikram into joining him for a meal in a Park Street restaurant. Normally, it would be unthinkable for a professional manager to be eating at the same table with a truck driver. But Kirpal was different. He had saved Vikram's life. Besides, he was on the way up. He was emigrating to the U.S. He was also wearing a pretty expensive suit, and appeared to be flush with money. Who would say he was a lowly truck driver?

"I'm not going back there either," said Vikram. "I have stopped going to the gardens even for the company audits. I refuse to be thrown to the wolves by our board of directors. It's all very well for them to sit in Dalhousie Square and reject the workers' demands. For them it's a minor side-show. Why don't they go to the gardens and refuse the workers face to face? That's because I'm expendable and they're not. But I've really nothing to fear from the laborers and the trade unionists. Everyone knows that the people who can give concessions are all in the Head Office in Calcutta. I too no longer have any qualms about throwing the red salute and crying 'Long Live Chairman Mao.'"

As their car slowly turned into Park Street, the shaded neons, the less than elegant store windows, and the city's rich came into focus. Women, some alone and others with company, walked with conspicuous poise in their tight *kameezes* and *churidars*. When the occasional couple paused in front of a sidewalk bookseller and the woman considered a film or fashion magazine, her male companion would quickly pass his gaze over the covers of the adult stuff. Perhaps it would be too embarrassing for him to bend down and actually pick one up publicly. Fat ladies wrapped breathlessly in *saris* tried to decide where to go for ice-cream and coffee. There were men and women rhythmically chewing their after-dinner *pan*, mouths oozing with red saliva, and women baring convulsive rolls of flesh round their carefree midriffs. Vendors sat on empty crates beside their stalls of cigarettes, chocolates, soda, bubble gum and condoms, coolly measuring each passer-by and anticipating each sale. Rickshaws waited for the odd sailor stumbling out of bars, students out for kicks, or well known regulars. The tubercular rickshaw pullers knew every one of the decaying pleasure domes around Free School Street.

The car moved slowly through the traffic. The people began to look all the same. Glossy lipstick, same hairstyles, the same vacant looks. The supposedly sexy, half-open, half-pouting Bardot-style mouth also seemed much in vogue with teenagers and younger women. The men in the dark suits looked the same too. Tall men with their condescending stoops, the short ones wearing the latest elevated heels, many with their hair combed down on their foreheads to hide the tell-tale signs of middle age and worse. Only the Marwaris, perhaps on account of a characteristic greasiness and rotundity, stood apart.

Kirpal Singh couldn't hide his curiosity any longer. "So the American woman decided to stay back?" he asked.

"Only for the time being," replied Vikram. "Only so she can look after Malini for a while. She's a great help with her studies."

Kirpal Singh started to laugh again. "You Bengalis will never get education out of your system. What's the point of going to college, especially for women? As for men, look at us."

"Not everybody is as enterprising as the Sikhs," said

Vikram patiently. "In India at least you're a nobody if you don't go to college."

"What for?" asked Kirpal facetiously. "They've boarded up all the colleges, haven't they?"

"I know what you mean," said Vikram, now smiling. "I hate to think what'll happen to our students this year and in the future. They keep postponing examinations one after the other, and when the university gets them going they're a farce anyway. Why blame the corporations when they discriminate against Bengalis where the best jobs are concerned. Why shouldn't they be partial to South Indians who toil like buffaloes or Punjabis who never know the difference between black and white, right and wrong?"

Kirpal, from the Punjab himself, joined in the laughter. The students had nothing to lose, he said, since eighty per cent of them would remain unemployed anyway. What the communists wanted was to make this unemployment total, right across the ranks of the educated. Then they expected all hell to break loose. Kirpal hoped the Prime Minister would see this threat and step out of her perennial palace and family intrigues.

"Isn't it a shame," lamented Vikram, "Her son has gone and ruined his chances by marrying an Italian. Met her in an English university town, Cambridge," he explained. "If only he had married a Greek, the stupid boy. She could've easily passed off as a descendant of Alexander the Great. A Greek princess would've been such a great idea, just what the people want. But Rajiv had to go and spoil it all."

"You need to be light-headed to be an airline pilot,"

suggested Kirpal, "or the airplane won't get off the ground."

The driver dropped them off in front of the Hole-in-the-Wall Restaurant and pulled away in search of a parking spot. The band hit them with a swinging blast as soon as they entered the place. Vikram was blinking and adjusting his eyes to the smoke and the dim lights when he was startled by a tap on his shoulder. "Hi there!" said a sexy voice, "haven't we met somewhere?"

Vikram turned around but failed to recognize the pretty woman who had spoken. She obviously didn't need to wait for an answer, for he saw her quickly withdraw into the crowd.

"*Arey wah*! what a bitch," exclaimed Kirpal, observing the woman. "These girls here are all the same. You won't find a decent one here."

When they saw her on the dance floor moments later, they felt sorry for her. There she was, her partner pressing relentlessly at her indestructible bosom with a sixty inch waist whose plastic convexity molded itself precisely against her body. They got to their table just as the band brought down the house with a rousing rendition of the theme from 'Butch Cassidy and the Sundance Kid.'

Other popular songs followed. The crooner, a sultry Anglo-Indian, her bejeweled body stuffed dangerously in a sheath of dazzling white satin, clutched the mike in her hand and swayed sensuously to the music. Her mind seemed far away, maybe with her fortunate friends who had got their immigration visas to Australia, Canada or England. So far away that she hardly seemed to notice the cord trailing from the mike down her soft belly to be caressed by the insides of her thighs with every undulation of her hips. Kirpal ordered Coke. After he had gulped down a couple of quick drinks, Vikram couldn't help expressing the vulgar hope, for Kirpal's benefit, that the cord would soon glow redhot and skewer her till she fainted in a quivering rapture. Kirpal thought it was really funny. They were beginning to chat like old friends.

"Will your little girl never be able to see?"

"The doctors think there's some hope for her," replied Vikram, "but only if we're prepared to take the risks."

Kirpal Singh knew something about the story surrounding Krishna and discreetly avoided the subject. They lapsed into silence. It took some effort to shout over the noise to be heard. Kirpal reflected that it wasn't easy to live with good eyes. "No, not easy at all," agreed Vikram. "I've often wondered what we might accomplish for Malini."

"When I was young, I was grateful for my eyes," said Kirpal. "Now that I've seen what I have, I'm not sure I wouldn't be better off being blind. Of course, I'm only joking," he added quickly. "I hope it works out for your daughter."

Vikram stared hard into his drink and murmured, "If only my wife could see and recognize herself once more, if only she could talk to us in a language we can understand." The more he thought of her, the more scared he felt for Malini. She'd be a woman someday, but the house would be so inadequate for her, so empty. He saw her life taking a path which would surely deny her all those experiences which make some sense out of living and dying. Malini would lose out. "The only advantage her blindness gives her," said Vikram, "is the power to discourage the high caste Brahmins of this city. They'll lust after my property but find no means of separating my daughter from her dowry."

"Unless they kill her," added Kirpal Singh, "after laying hands on your property. Happens all the time in the Punjab."

The band tripped along merrily, the undulating crooner shut her eyes and sang indifferently. Vikram grew more and more depressed. If she ever recovered her sight, he thought, would she not be disenchanted to discover her mother is locked up in a madhouse and her father is no more than a thriving mediocrity. "Can you believe it," he asked, looking up at Kirpal, "that two-thirds of my life is probably over, and all I have to show for it is garbage, piles of paper stuffed in trash-cans."

"We Sikhs may be stupid," said Kirpal, "but I don't think many people could've done better. We have a saying that many smiles, many pretended pleasures, simply hide the dried-up balls, the shriveled dugs, and hollow minds."

There was something desperate about the way Vikram was pouring his heart out to a stranger. The man had saved his life. Could it be that he might save his mind as well?

"You should come away to America too," said Kirpal, before leaving. "I'm ignorant and uneducated. We'll remain that way wherever we are. People like you can do anything you want."

Vikram drove to his father's house to take Malini home. Under the mellow lights in their family room, Sir Ajoy was telling her a story. "I won't be too long," said his father, as he continued with the story to his audience of one, clinging to every word.

Vikram eased himself into the sofa next to where Malini was lying with her face resting in her hands, deaf to everything but the story. His mood of despondency deepened even further. He had a blissfully happy marriage once upon a time. Again he chided himself for having little to show for the seven years of their lives. He couldn't teach her to survive, not in seven years of marriage, while this contagion of pain spread through his mind and hers. Yet, it wasn't so in the beginning. What went wrong? Where did they fail each other? At the time he married Krishna he was obsessed with a vague craving for detachment. It sounded good, but what did detachment mean? It was shattering to discover now he had all along been moving blindly in circles of self-pity and indulgence.

fifteen

As she grew more anxious about Krishna, Janaki Devi began to travel more frequently between Bishnupur and Calcutta. Vikram even suggested she leave Bishnupur altogether, since Rahul was obviously around even though he hadn't often come back to the village after the one visit when he had been sick. She smiled wistfully and said that instead of settling down in the city she'd always stay with Vikram and Krishna when she was visiting, rather than with his parents as she had in the past. So she came to her daughter whenever Krishna felt a little better and was allowed home from the hospital.

Although Rahul encouraged his mother to stay as long as possible in Calcutta, her visits were in fact getting shorter and shorter. Krishna seemed unable to stay home for more than a week or two without having to go back to the hospital for therapy.

Every time, during the first few days of her visit, Janaki Devi found Krishna irrepressible, speaking continually, pacing the floor all the time. Such spells, such bursts of energy, would soon fade away. She found it difficult to keep pace with Krishna's thoughts during these spells.

"I can't understand you anymore, Krishna," she said one day. "You seem to find all this so oppressive. Don't you like staying with us anymore?"

"But mother," replied Krishna, "I do, I do. It's the doors I hate coming back to, and the windows, and the roof over my head, and the walls that surround me."

Tears came to Janaki Devi's eyes as Krishna fell silent. Slowly, she left the chair and walked to the window where the sunlight poured richly over her face, forcing her to move away. "Then you must hate me too," she said, "for how is my life any different from a door through which people are always walking away?" The sadness in her voice went unnoticed by Krishna. She didn't seem to understand her mother's mind any more than her mother understood hers.

"But it is you who are walking away from me," she said, asking her mother to try to listen and understand. "How can I explain to you that I don't hate you, or anyone? But I do feel sorry for you, just as I feel a little sorry for father. You brought him his tea to bed, stood around while he finished his meals, ironed his shirts, yelled at his servants. Now that he's gone, and most of the servants too, all you do is pray to your gods all day. Nothing will change for you, mother. Neither your prayers, nor mine, will make the smallest difference to the world. It will creak away as before, pushing us into the kitchen and the bedroom.

Forgive me if I turn away from your clay gods. I wish I could do it without hurting you. What difference will one more wound mean to you? Where do you find your strength? Maybe in the very terror of life's mindless blows as day turns to night and night to sleep. I need sleep too. It won't matter to me if I never wake up again.

"But then I want to turn night into day, blazing with the heat of wrath, striking down the weak and the mute, the deaf and the blind. Yes, I've found a god too, the God of Destruction. The other, the Giver, has given too much to too few. His time has run out. I'll hunt him through my dark night till he flies away from the forest on swift wings to where gods are supposed to be. Where? Your eyes seem to ask me. Who knows. But let him seed the clouds with pain, and plant defiance, not hope, in human hearts. If I ever nurse again, let me nurse pain, not babies. If a man should ever fire my passion again, let his sighs be those of the lost, his pleasure that of the damned."

Krishna stopped, exhausted, and looked around with frightened eyes. "You're less than human, mother," she whispered after a while. "A puppet on a string. A bit like father too. You cry and it makes me laugh. You pray and I feel bored. You know Death will wear you out like our temples by the sea, hollow shells where the lamp no longer burns, which the priest no longer enters. I'll not leave till my screams have struck terror in men's hearts, not till I have gouged out the festering soul of man. Oh mother! you think I rant in my madness, but do you not hear the others? There are others who sleep that join me in a chorus. The living will never hear or comprehend our voices."

Janaki Devi was unable to fully understand her daughter.

Still, she believed in her wisdom that the words had less to do with her than with a world which tramples and enslaves, all for the price of living. It was a world she loathed too, but Krishna hadn't noticed that. Stumbling in the dark, reaching out for shadows, perhaps discovering stars ringed round her fingers, tiptoeing on the moon trapped in the rain-soaked terrace, Krishna already seemed part of a kingdom out of bounds to most mortals.

It was at this moment that Malini burst into the room. She turned her face in the direction of her mother's voice and waited for some acknowledgement of her presence, some words of welcome. Like everyone else in the family, she too had learned to accept her mother's brief visits to the house as natural, so that when it came time for her to go away Malini no longer showed any great emotion. She knew it simply meant that Janaki Devi too would return to Bishnupur, and she'd go back to spending her days with her other grandmother and her study hours with Alice.

Finding no response from Krishna, Malini advanced towards her grandmother, crying, "The monkey man is here. The monkey man is here." She grasped Janaki Devi's hand and pulled her excitedly out of the room. Krishna took a few uncertain steps behind her mother. Then she changed her mind and walked back to the window.

"Alice, Alice, come quickly," she cried, as she dragged her Grandma down the stairs. Alice heard her and rushed out of her room.

Down below, in front of the house, the monkey man was already at work, a stick in one hand, a drum in the other. Two little monkeys pranced to his drumbeats, each wearing a pair of pants, a red shirt, and a red, embroidered cap. They balanced themselves on little blocks of wood, nodded their heads in answer to the monkey man's questions, held each other's hands and danced, pretended to be angry with one another, and finally agreed to marry and live happily ever after. A small crowd of children and servants from neighboring houses stood outside the gate and watched the monkey man perform. Janaki Devi and Malini stood on the front verandah. Malini was quite content to let her imagination run wild at the sound of the drumbeats and the monkey man's voice.

Suddenly, there came the noise of glass shattering somewhere inside the house. A shower of glass splinters came down on the front lawn, barely missing the monkey man and his monkeys. The show stopped. The spectators on the other side of the gate, the monkey man and the servants, everyone strained their eyes towards the upstairs window where the pane had shattered. As soon as she recovered from the shock, Janaki Devi let go of Malini's hand and rushed back into the house. She hurried up the stairs to where she had left Krishna. Alice was already there, holding Krishna's head in her lap. She lay directly in front of the shattered window, blood oozing gently from an angry gash across her forehead. It looked like she was in the throes of one of her seizures. The shattered glass was the one flawed pane Vikram had wanted to have replaced for many years, but had never gotten round to.

It was quite dark by the time Vikram returned home after checking Krishna in at the hospital. His father returned with him too. At the sight of Sir Ajoy, Janaki Devi quickly covered her head with her *sari*. It was a gesture of modesty and deference she never overlooked at any time. Sir Ajoy folded his hands and greeted her silently. Janaki Devi hovered near the door, waiting for Vikram to say something. She seemed disappointed he had so little to say. "She's all right now." That was all he had to say.

It was time for Janaki Devi to return home. Her heart went out to Malini. For her sake she would stay a few days longer. Lady Ranu and Sir Ajoy insisted that she do so. Inwardly, they were both terrified of what the future held for Malini. Janaki Devi's company gave them some comfort. So did Alice's presence.

Sir Ajoy was at an age when people look away from the future and its uncertainties. They find it much more pleasurable to muse over the past than poke around in the shadows of the valley of death and disease. He liked to think of his own childhood as having been exciting, carefree, even wicked. He was saddened to think Malini's life would end someday without similar happy memories of youth. In the evening, when Vikram's car waited to take Malini back home, Sir Ajoy often saw him lead his daughter into the dusk and remembered his own childhood. The dusks of his younger days were woven with memories of a lovable, if eccentric, school headmaster.

Every evening, the headmaster would choose a boy or two to walk with along the riverbank. As he walked, he would tell them stories of Newton, Shivaji, Socrates, Aurangzeb, Napoleon, Alexander, Buddha, and Christ. Sir Ajoy remembered there was nothing scary about the man on the riverbank, as there was in school during the day when everyone looked upon him with fear. Beside the river, the students felt proud and privileged.

Sir Ajoy remembered once visiting the headmaster with his partners in crime, quaking with fear, waiting for the straps to follow the two bottles of lemonade they had removed from the headmaster's house, drunk too quickly, and slept too late the next morning. The strap again for decorating the chocolate soufflé with brown shoepolish. But not for the time he set fire to part of the schoolhouse while trying to destroy an infamous black notebook. That was another story.

It was all accidental, of course. In the notebook were the dreaded records of extreme misconduct. Sir Ajoy, a good student whom the headmaster did not wish to lose, had already found two dishonorable mentions there. One more entry would've meant suspension and the end of his chances of appearing in the matriculation exams only two months away. But when his friend Satish told him that the zamindar's *durwan* across the river had refused them access to the *lichi* trees, he was incensed. It was a signal to throw caution to the winds.

The next Saturday night they crossed the river in a borrowed boat and set about the *lichi* trees in earnest. It was only after they had loaded the boat with their loot that their presence was discovered. The snapping twigs and the rustling leaves had given them away. Soon there were at least a dozen men combing the trees with flashlights and hurricane lanterns. One of the men recognized the boys as they leapt out of the branches and ran for the river. The boat capsized and the *lichi*s spilled into the river. Sir Ajoy and Satish managed to swim across in the dark.

A complaint from the zamindar, a third entry in the black book, and suspension was guaranteed. From morning till noon Sunday, Ajoy and Satish went without food and worried themselves sick. Finally, after much planning, they went to the village and got two more bottles of lemonade. "Well, maybe something a little stronger than lemonade," Sir Ajoy corrrected himself when questioned closely by Malini. And maybe the boat was borrowed without permission.

Later that evening, when the caretaker had gone to sleep after drinking too much lemonade and his wife was busy baking chappatis on the fire, Ajoy slipped out of the caretaker's room with his keys. With two friends helping, he opened the headmaster's office and held a lighted match to the black book in a corner of the room. With the flames reasonably high, they unlocked one of the windows and slipped back into the caretaker's room. They quickly raised an alarm and became heroes for saving the school from destruction. When the zamindar's complaint came in the following day, Ajoy and Satish were solemnly censured for trespassing and some minor transgression. But it was all recorded in a brand new black book. They were home free.

The growing tension between father and son could not however be kept in check for too long. It rose to the surface one day, catching them both unawares. Sir Ajoy looked worried as the confrontation began. He furrowed his brow deeply in a supreme effort at concentration. His face always assumed this expression whenever he had something important on his mind. He'd continue to look this way until he had said what needed to be said. The lamp, he said, was too bright for the room. He turned his eyes away from it and asked, "So what have you decided to do about Malini?"

"What do you mean?" asked Vikram, surprised.

"What I mean is that she's growing up," said Sir Ajoy impatiently. "What are your plans for giving her a chance to lead a normal life?"

Vikram's surprise gave way to irritation. "But she seems quite happy with mother during the day."

"You know damn well she's not," snapped Sir Ajoy. "And don't pretend that your mother enjoys it any more than she does. The same with Malini. From the moment your car drops her off here during the day, all she can think of is your return in the evening. Come six o'clock, and she may be waiting all by herself, waiting for the sound of your car, waiting to return to Alice. I think she hates it here."

"Are you suggesting that I give up my job and stay home with her all day?"

Sir Ajoy chose to ignore the unmistakable edge in his son's voice. "I simply wanted to remind you," he said, "of what the specialists said several years ago. That they might be able to do something for her eyes once she was older. Why don't you call on some of them again? Take her to Moscow. They say there's an eye surgeon there performing a hundred miracles each day."

"All right," said Vikram dryly. "I'll check them out."

"Get a hold of yourself." Sir Ajoy's voice rose with his ebbing patience. "You're not the only one who has suffered, you know. We've all suffered with you. We're suffering with you every moment of our lives. Are you blind? Can you not see others?

Others who have been less fortunate than you and me. Learn to face facts. Use the strengths you have."

Words, words, thought Vikram. When excited, they were always so good with words. Even when there was no hope and all was lost, there were words. That he deserved this homily, he didn't doubt. What an awful mess his life was in. All his ideas, promises, hopes, all wasted. He had hardly bothered to move them around, to look at them, from the day Alice had made up her mind to leave.

He hadn't tried to reason with her. The chains that held them together for a while had snapped. If she was staying on for a while longer, it was almost by default, more for the love of Malini and Krishna than anything else. Not that he didn't miss his earlier closeness to her, missed it all the more now that he had lost Krishna a second time. He could also live with the slight pangs of jealousy he felt when she went up to Bishnupur with Janaki Devi one day, and stayed back for weeks to nurse Rahul back to health.

Every day, the house was growing larger, emptier, utterly devoid of warmth. Suddenly the odds seemed stacked too high against Malini, the empty spaces in the house too large to be filled up. Malini would tinker with the piano in the evenings, but that was no substitute for a woman's voice or the sound of her laughter.

Sir Ajoy kept looking at him for an answer. Vikram's silence turned deeper and deeper inwards. Yes, he would revert to his bachelor days, thought Vikram. He had already come close to it in many ways. How he hated messing around with the price of fish and the size of the tomatoes. Hadn't he already started to order the daily bazaar most days? He was even beginning to find some interest in the affairs of the cook who was as brilliant under proper supervision as he was a disaster without it. He knew the cook resented his new-found interest in the kitchen, and the servants sneered as he snooped around for cobwebs on the ceiling and dust on the bookshelves.

It was not as if he hadn't been thinking of Malini while he was changing his ways. He wished his father could take note of that. Malini loved good food. Malini hated objects that were dusty. Yes, now there was something else he had to get up and do for her. Who but his father had the right to advise him? He probably should be fairer, he told himself. Indeed, his father had seldom told him how to run his life. Could he have known that all his son wanted to be was a poet? God knows he tried hard enough. Krishna once said how nice it would be to have him home all day composing verses. He worked hard, wrote hundreds of lines, then ripped them all up one day. He had never tried since. The feelings had all dried up inside his soul.

At times he reminded himself the trouble with most of us is that we ignore ourselves as artists. In not recognizing the artist within while it is flesh and blood, we abort it swiftly and permanently, then spend the rest of our lives miscasting ourselves in roles destined for others. Never satisfied, we soon get used to pretending. While he worked all day to ward off pain, to be nice, to brush the specks of age off his face, was it not wonderful that Krishna should be above it all? Surely, of all the places on earth, an asylum might be the one place where sanity was most abundant. The walls of thought crumble, its paths choke up with brambles, and all at once we are face to face with a mind that's naked and vulnerable, but unconquerable. If it raves and froths at the mouth, is it not expressing a reality we often feel ourselves?

Every time he saw Krishna's inscrutable face, he felt ashamed of the pretensions we encourage in others and glorify in ourselves. Maybe she's happy. Who can tell? With all our ingenuity, we still hadn't figured out what happiness is, let alone know for certain where to find it. Krishna had probably found that which we were destined to find one day. She had found her way out of a crazy world that shuts out light and shuts away those who might've seen it. Maybe she was in the same wilderness as her father.

Is it better for Krishna where she is? He asked himself. If there's a God, perhaps this was his way of preparing us to face him, wants, needs and desires overpowered, logic blown to the winds, pride humbled. How else could one explain the man awaiting death with impatience, or another courting it with passion? They're either deranged at the moment before death, or all their ambition and cruelty, the endless search for satisfaction, self-preservation, all these were symptoms of a strange madness. The soldier who religiously takes his antibiotics or whatever before venturing into brothels can't surely be the man who charges a blazing gun with his bayonet.

Yes, he knew all about death. He had seen it since he was a boy. He had seen men scream in terror on their deathbed, eyes stark and wide open. Perhaps that was sanity staring out of this man's eyes. He protests against the crushing of the living soul, this abrupt rebuff at the banquet. He tries to come to terms with an idiotic anti-climax. He's convinced there has been a terrible mistake. Vikram had also known others who walked to death in ignorance, their pride strutting till the very end. If they weren't afraid, was it because they imagined the confrontation to be a big joke? Did they know that the joke might lead to unexpected twists and turns?

He wondered if the man rejoicing at the onrush of death might be suffering from a surfeit of spiritual ecstasy rather than madness. It could just be that the seeker of the true, the good, and the beautiful had at last found journey's end. What earthly reason could he have to rave and cry in terror? Perhaps that was it. His reasons must be unearthly. The seeker of the truth, if he had been sane to start with, would've blown his brains out long ago to be transported swiftly to journey's end. Either that, or he was a fool. Must've been incorrigibly mad to have waited a lifetime. Either one accepted this, or that he was mad to extend a welcome to death. One couldn't otherwise explain the odd contradiction from which we avert our eyes for fear of the unknown. The same vantage point couldn't offer a vindication of both life and death. There had to be a reversal of fond beliefs, a change in posture.

Somehow, he couldn't help envying Krishna. Painful, yes. But the process of separation seemed to have been so subtle for her. He thanked God she was beyond the reach of those who might have tried to restore and prolong what he was certain was no more than a dubious sanity. Even those maimed or blinded like Malini stood a better chance of finding a simple end, a simple meaning, to life. In them, the fire was already enfeebled, the promises hazy, the grand meanings almost useless. It seemed so much easier to walk away from trails that led nowhere.

Vikram made up his mind to be pleasant to his father. Lady Ranu came in to say dinner was served. Vikram smiled. "I'm sorry, father," he said gently, "I'll look up the specialists soon." Sir Ajoy looked transfigured with happiness.

sixteen

WHENEVER VIKRAM and Malini left his father's house, it was time for her to come out with her complaints for the day. "I wish Granma wouldn't keep moving the furniture all the time," she said that evening. "I'm always bumping into things. I told her I'd break my leg someday and then she'd be stuck with me for the rest of her life." Malini giggled happily as she described how angry this made Lady Ranu. Vikram ruffled up her hair and added to her amusement.

Malini asked one evening if Alice would take her to another symphony someday. When Vikram replied he wasn't sure if there'd be another recital before she left, she became depressed. "I wish she wouldn't go," she said. She had often said the same thing to Alice who assured her she'd be all right.

"You'll be all grown up and beautiful when I see you again. I've been here so long, all my work is piling up back home.

We don't have any servants, you see." It hadn't sounded very convincing to Malini. She didn't look forward to kissing Alice goodbye.

"Is Mama still very ill?" she asked one day. She brightened up when Vikram told her she was much better and said she might be home again soon. Although Vikram promised her Krishna would be home as soon as the doctors let her, it was getting to be a long, long time. Now, every time Malini raised her hopes about her mother returning home, she felt less sure of herself. Her doubts and suspicions grew each day. Vikram felt her stifled need for Krishna surprising him through unexpected questions and situations. He felt quite helpless at times in his need to draw upon all his reserves of tact and delicacy to avoid mutual embarrassment. Once Alice left, he knew the questions would be difficult to avoid.

Krishna still didn't come home, and Malini decided she ought to visit her. She asked Vikram quite directly why she couldn't visit her mother at the hospital. Why couldn't he take her for just a few minutes when he went himself? She promised not to say a word. Trying to make her plea even stronger, she said, "After I've been with her a little while, I'll go and sit quietly in the car if you want me to." Alice wanted to accompany them too, but couldn't get herself to ask.

"Is it all right if I bring my daughter to see my wife someday?" Vikram asked the superintendent of the asylum.

In reply, he received a complicated answer riddled with uncertainties. "In your wife's case, such a visit might produce a desirable therapeutic effect," said the superintendent. "Then again, it might not. We can't really say anything for certain. You see, we've still to come up with a satisfactory prognosis."

Vikram thanked the man for the great help he had been. He had seen visitors bring children to the place, so he couldn't see what harm could come to either Malini or Krishna if they were to meet during one of his visits. Malini might draw from Krishna some token of recognition. At worst, she'd be greeted with icy silence.

When they finally met in the asylum one day, Vikram was shocked to notice how Krishna had aged, how devastated she looked next to Malini. He no longer believed there was any hope left for her. She had lost so much weight her flesh hung loosely under her chin and on her arms. Gone were the little soft mounds on her cheeks, gone the softness of the temples that retained an impression long after caressing fingers broke off their touch. The skin on her face was tightly drawn, dry and cracked. Her thinning hair was tied behind her head with a frayed, oily string.

She sat silently in a posture of meditation. Then she suddenly became voluble, reciting and elaborating on some poems of Sudhin Dutta, her favorite Bengali poet. True to her promise, Malini didn't utter a word as Vikram sat her on a wooden chair. Malini sat quietly in the chair, occasionally shifting her weight from one side to the other. But the chair's legs were uneven. Every time she moved, the chair moved up and down as well, the sound of the wood hitting the floor reverberating through the pauses in the aimless conversation. It added to the other noises one heard from time to time, and turned the air heavy and oppressive. Unable to stand it any longer, and hoping to distract Malini, Vikram tried to think of things to say.

"I'm glad to see you're looking well, Krishna." He sounded foolish and desperate. "I hope mother finishes your cardigan before winter's over." He said other things too, before giving up altogether. Not a muscle flickered on Krishna's face to suggest she had heard anything. She was deaf to his niceties. Soon, her earlier exuberance dried up completely. Sudhin Dutta lay far behind, forgotten, as if she had suddenly run out of words. "Where's my notebook?" she suddenly said distractedly. She kept looking from side to side.

Vikram too looked around the room, on the one table and a single drawer, in a small closet which held her clothes. He found nothing, no signs of a notebook. By the time he had finished, it seemed Krishna no longer cared.

Malini knew where Krishna's bed stood. She knew too that it she had only reached forward from her chair she might have even touched her mother. She looked bewildered, unsure of the reaction a touch might give rise to. As they walked back to the car, she asked, "Did she not see me at all?"

Vikram said nothing in reply. Once inside the car, he drew Malini close to himself and asked if she would like to see her mother again.

"Yes," she replied, sounding confused, "if you'll bring me when she's a little better."

Vikram didn't take Malini to the hospital anymore. Even his own visits no longer served any purpose. They seemed so mechanical, more for the sake of propriety than remembered love. Once there was plenty of sentiment in him, and he equated it with his love. Now that he felt pity for Krishna, but not love, he wondered if that sentiment might've been replaced by sensibility. He was worried to think he was developing an unnatural streak in his character. Never a very complicated person, his mental needs had always been those of the average, his responses simple. But as he now looked for an emotional response to Krishna, he found none and grew alarmed over his weak and inconsequential feelings.

Lately, Vikram often found himself brooding over Krishna's last pregnancy. He confessed to me one day how suspicious he had been for a time, how confused and resentful. Maybe it was not his child after all. In retrospect, he was glad it ended the way it did. But he couldn't help wondering if his suspicions had anything to do with the erosion of his love for Krishna. Was there really something abrupt and sudden about it? Erosion and decay were two words that kept repeating themselves in his mind. They were also words that seemed to describe the process by which Krishna had ceased to exist. But the spirits who now lent their breath to her, in exchange for her mind, felt no concern for him. Why couldn't they teach him something of her language?

Vikram had finished dinner alone. Malini was in bed, and so was Alice. The servants had locked up and gone. When the telephone suddenly began to ring that night, Vikram was afraid to touch it. It was the asylum. What could the superintendent want at this hour of the night? The instrument grew heavy in his hand. "Yes, I'm Vikram Mukherjee," he said, in answer to a question from the other end.

"Will you please come immediately," asked the superintendent, his voice shaking with nervousness.

"What's the matter?"

"I'm afraid there has been a terrible accident."

Vikram was surprised how quickly he was in control of himself. "Is she alive or dead?" he asked quietly.

There was a moment's pause at the other end. "Barely alive."

Vikram opened a door and stepped out into the terrace. The night was cold and the stars pushed and shoved against one another for a berth in the sky. He stood there for a long time and gradually grew certain he would never see Krishna again.

He closed the door as he stepped back into the house and slumped down on the sofa. He felt overcome by a feeling not unlike that which follows sustained effort once the goal is reached. But so little had been achieved in his case. He'd have to get up, change, take out the car. It seemed like a major undertaking. He lacked even the energy to get his feet to stand up.

The prospect of future loneliness filled him with some anxiety. During Krishna's illness, he had invested single-mindedly in isolation and even relished it sometimes. It was different then. Krishna was alive. He felt no desire at this stage of his life to forge new ties, cultivate new friendships, in the hope they'd endure. He didn't think such a venture would be difficult or impossible. He simply lacked the heart to try.

He would make America his new home, he thought. Return

to books. To poetry. There was a time when he thought of moving in with his parents to make full use of the magnificent library in the old house. Not anymore. It would please his father immensely, he thought, to have a scholar, a savant, for a son. He wasn't quite sure how they'd respond to a poet. Did his family not suffer in comparison with some of the other aristocratic Bengali families precisely because it lacked an artist of any stature? He would fill this void. He would harness whatever creative forces still remained in him and publish a book or two, slim volumes of collected poems. In the thirty-seventh year of his life, he, Vikram Mukherjee, scion of the Mukherjee's of Uttarpara, ex family man, intermediary between the past and the future, would close shop and turn to culture. He'd create a cultural fortress in America. Let detractors say what they will.

But if all that failed, thought Vikram, could he ever be as circumspect as his father? Would he be able to persuade himself to prune rose bushes, to smoke a pipe behind closed windows and watch the rain lashing the panes? Could he condense his life from January to December into a faultless card-index system? Roast beef and Yorkshire pudding on Sundays. Grilled *beckti* on Thursdays. Canned apricots and vanilla ice cream for dessert on Saturday nights. Old shoes on the topmost shelf of the closet. New shoes lined on the floor to the right. Old and new shoes both to be aired on the first Sunday each month. Blankets not to be lifted out of their moth-balled limbo before the fifteenth day of November, not unless pneumonia set in earlier from unexpected exposure. Could Vikram ever be one with people who wither inside and grow leathery on the surface? An uncomplicated man, he was glad to brush aside these questions for the time being. Instead, he peered into the day that lay ahead and prepared himself to face its needs one more time. They seemed more complicated and demanding now that Krishna lay dying.

"Not again," he groaned as he heard the telephone ringing. He had almost fallen asleep. He shook himself awake and started walking towards the phone. For one fleeting moment, he thought it might be Krishna. The phone kept on ringing. As he passed the large window of the living room, he, looked out into the night, saw the stars, and remembered.

"The ambulance is on its way to here," cried the superintendent's anxious voice.

"Yes, yes, I'm coming," said Vikram and hung up.

He let the cold water run for some time before he splashed it on his face. The cologne, the lavender water, the bath salts, the deodorants, they were all on the shelf exactly as Krishna had left them. Vikram poured out some cologne and rubbed it on his wet face. Then he entered his room and switched on the light. He was surprised to see Malini curled up between the pillows on his bed. He pulled out a fresh shirt from the closet and walked softly out of the room. He waited in the corridor to make sure he hadn't woken her up, then closed the door behind him.

The superintendent rushed out to meet him as soon as he stepped into the courtyard. He was barely able to keep the tears off his face. "They've just taken her to the hospital," he said, "what little there's left of her."

Vikram's first impulse was to walk back to the car and head for the hospital. He felt ashamed for having taken so long to respond to the superintendent's call. But he decided to walk to Krishna's room instead. An invisible force kept pushing him in that direction.

In the corner of the courtyard near Krishna's room, there stood three short women, doing nothing. At that hour of the night, it was strange to see them there, just standing. There was something ugly and frightening about them. Outside Krishna's door, a young man dressed impeccably in white sat on the floor, furiously turning the pages of a thick book covered with brown paper. Two uniformed police officers followed Vikram onto the verandah. The young man in white looked up apprehensively as he heard the approaching footsteps. He shut his book violently, stood up, and ran away. Vikram walked wordlessly, without showing any emotion. The grieving superintendent kept striking his forehead with his hand. His tears flowed freely. Vikram couldn't help feeling sorry for the man. "You've done your best," he said, trying to comfort the superintendent.

The wet, empty bed stared back at Vikram as soon as they entered the room. He could see the burnt patches on the mattress and places where the wooden bed itself was charred. "They must've put out the fire quickly enough," remarked one police officer to the other.

Vikram walked slowly round the bed, picking his feet carefully on the wet floor. A stab of pain crossed his heart as he realized this was where she lay only a short while ago, his wife. But the pain was momentary. As he took another step, he felt his shoes tread over something soft. Vikram bent down to find a spray of red oleanders. He felt sad he had unwittingly crushed the flowers. It was fitting, he thought, that Krishna should think of dying with a token which had once moved her so deeply. She seemed always to have lived only an arm's length away from violence and death. It surprised him to think she had survived so long and so tenuously.

Krishna continued to linger. Over at the hospital, Vikram didn't know why they had laid her out on a bed of fresh leaves. No doubt the doctors knew what they were doing, he thought, as he saw the huge banana leaves spread between her body and the mattress. Over her body was a semi-circular cage, a kind of shell covered with a faded white sheet. Through an opening on one side of the shell, Krishna's head jutted out like an inert object splashed with grease.

Vikram found a nurse sitting by the bed, fanning it with a sheaf of folded newspapers. As he approached her, the nurse stood up and left the tiny cubicle. Instantly, there were hordes of flies swarming over Krishna's face. Vikram brought his face close to hers so he might blow the flies away. He took a deep breath and almost choked. Krishna's body was rotting. It was as if masses of molten wax had guttered past her eyes and congealed over her ears. Blind with pity and rage, Vikram reached out into the cage for Krishna's hand and whispered, "Look, Krishna, I've come to see you."

Her open eyes lay fixed in a pool of blisters, glassy and lustrous over her blackened face. Not a muscle moved. Not an eyelash flickered. Her upper lip had fused with the tip of her nose which was now level with her swollen cheeks. The lower lip, stretched taut below an even set of teeth, trembled ever so slightly. The movement might've been wholly in his imagination, but it did seem to him at the time that Krishna was trying to say something.

Conscious of nothing but the flies, and trying to touch Krishna's hand, Vikram pushed his own hand further under the edge of the shell. It was surprisingly light. He would discover later that it was made of galvanized wire and used exclusively for severe burn victims. His fingers inched forward through that stinking void until his nails scraped against something hard and moist Vikram drew his hand away instantly, only to rub against something else, soft, cold, and jelly-like. It was strange and fearful. Some unseen force seemed to be reshaping Krishna's pliant body, perhaps preparing, he thought in passing, for the proverbial needle's eye.

Vikram looked foolishly at his hand and the specks of blood and flesh clinging to his fingers. Just then, the nurse returned. Vikram became aware of her presence only after she had spoken. She was unemotional, quite matter of fact. "I should've warned you," she said. As she spoke, she casually lifted up the sheet covering the shell. "Take a look," she said. "It's only a matter of time now."

There was a small light bulb hooked inside the top of the shell. Vikram saw everything in a flash. "Thank you," he murmured in a choked voice, looking away. Then he walked away into the night, leaving the divine cook to garnish Krishna's body in his finest culinary tradition.

When he reached home, there seemed nothing Vikram could do to stop himself from sniffing his fingers. Every time he did so, it sent through his nostrils the smell of Krishna's half cooked body. Within the day, he had developed a curious, bothersome habit, He tried washing with detergents, Dettol, mustard oil, kerosene, milk. He rubbed his fingers with cologne, even mud. Nothing worked. Frantic, he even entertained the thought of eventually burning the skin off his fingers with acid or something equally toxic.

Usually, he had been quite good when it came to shaking off bad habits. This seemed more formidable. He remembered how it had taken him exactly one day to overcome the most compulsive one he'd ever had. It was after a particularly moving lecture delivered by Father Thomas in their final high school biology class. The priest had pulled himself to his full height and assumed a curious expression of piety and earnestness. The students could almost sense that a moment of truth was at hand. "I want you all to understand," he said, "why I've saved this last class for the subject of human reproduction. The reason is, short of union with God, the mating of the sexes is the most wonderful union man can hope for. God made sperm so the human race may move through the cleansing fires of the worst famines, plagues, and wars, and still endure to give glory to His mystery and greatness." He paused here, eyeing the students with suspicion, searching for signs of guilt. Finally, breaking into a bashful smile, he concluded abruptly by saying, "Don't waste the seed. It's a terrible sin."

Vikram recalled what a devastating effect those simple words had on him. He wept all night over his terrible sins and vowed he would never defile himself. He felt even more crushed after Father Laporte's beautiful lecture a few weeks later. The occasion was a Retreat, one of the surprising 'extras' which some Indian children received, regardless of caste, creed, or religion, simply by going to Christian schools.

Father Laporte conducted the Retreat every year for as long as one could remember. It was held before the graduating class left, as he put it, the portals of this sheltered life to be buffeted by a world of harsh realities. What a beautiful voice he had, thought Vikram, still washing himself.

"You are all men now," he had begun, pausing for effect. "There are few secrets in the world of men. The supreme secret is God, and him you must discover in your own hearts. We can only lead you by the hand so far, we can only pray for you. Beyond that, you're on your own. So place your trust in Him. It can be a lonely, terrifying odyssey if you don't."

Turning to the subject of sin, Father Laporte said, "Sin we will. Sin we may. But remember, God's arms are forever reaching out for you. In his ever-loving kindness, which, like Him, is infinite, all he demands of you is true repentance."

Vikram wondered if another obsessive spell of repentance was about to open up before him. How he had repented through those hours devoted to meditation and introspection. During a particularly savage fit of depression, he found himself on the verge of chopping off his right hand since he had lost count of the number of times it had caused him to sin. It was bitter remembering the countless occasions when, in his imagination, in closets, parks, and private gardens, he had dipped his burning fingers into the unholy slime of debauched girls and withdrawn them reeking of damnation and ammonia. Since the comforts of a confessional were beyond the reach of

Hindus, however rich or privileged, Vikram had contemplated going down to the school kitchen. There, he planned to pick up a deadly meat cleaver with his left hand and send it crashing on his right. As if that was not enough, Vikram even pictured himself presenting his severed hand to Father Laporte and seeking whatever absolution the Church was prepared to grant a heathen like him. It must have been God's will that he shrink from recourse to such drastic penance. Before anything dreadful could happen, God interrupted his macabre fantasies with the dinner gong. It sounded like His personal summons. Vikram had obeyed like a lamb.

Father Laporte left no stone unturned. Later, he was to speak to them on the subject of heaven, hell, birth control, and venereal disease. He gave his audience what seemed then to be a first hand and graphic account of the death of Herod Antipas, a figure familiar to the students from their study of the Gospels. He even declared strong empirical connections between contraception and cancer. For most of his students, for a long time to come, cancer became synonymous with sin. Vikram remembered how deeply moved he had been for a particularly close friend whose mother had died of uterine cancer only a few months ago. He liked her a lot and hoped she would somehow dodge the gates of hell. Not even Nehru at his most eloquent, speaking to thousands in the field in front of the school, ever matched the effect on Vikram of Father Laporte's penetrating discourse on sin.

It now seemed another life, alien and remote. Vikram wondered if he wasn't a bit of a hypocrite after all. Perhaps he should've exposed himself longer to prayers and the influence of priests. It was true he had tried to live a good, decent life. But he had also pretended to give glory to the mystery and greatness of God under conditions probably unimaginable to Fathers Thomas and Laporte.

Wiping his hands briskly with the last of the dry towels, Vikram concluded that these confounded notions came together only in his mind. It seemed silly to think there existed any connection between the sins of his past and the brutal end to his marriage. But somewhere at the back of his mind, a nagging voice was crying 'Punishment.' It kept haunting him even on the cremation grounds where they took Krishna the following day. What the voice seemed trying to tell him was that he deserved it all, even if he couldn't understand why.

There weren't many people at the funeral. A message had been sent to Bishnupur, but Janaki Devi did not come. Rahul still wasn't well enough to travel. There hardly seemed any need for Krishna's mother to pay this final visit to Calcutta. Women wouldn't normally attend a cremation anyway.

Then it was time to light the inevitable fire. Vikram stood up and prepared to join the others. He held the burning twigs with both hands while the priest poured *ghee* over the logs. The hour was late and all other sounds were stifled. The nearby streets and shops were all deserted. Only a few unseen birds flapped their wings in the trees on the bank. The priest's voice was deep and resonant in the night.

Vikram circled the pyre and stood still for a moment as he

touched Krishna's lips with the fire. The face came back to life to reveal a peace and forgiveness he had all but forgotten. Then it returned briefly to the night as he moved away and thrust the burning twigs into the logs.

Flames leapt up from the centre and swiftly spread to the sides. The priest was about to raise his voice in a final invocation, when we were all startled by the dark figure of a holy man, towering, almost regal, who came out of the night and walked right up to the burning pyre and knelt in front of it.

His long hair was twisted, not braided, into ropes that fell past his waist. Around his neck he wore long strands of heavy iron chains which jangled with every step he took. Through the mass of hair covering his face, only his eyes were visible in the darkness. Eyes on fire. With a deliberate and powerful thrust of his hand, the holy man planted his trident in the soft earth. He closed his eyes, clasped his hands together in prayer, and began to chant:

> Take this body, O burning fire,
> Turn it to ashes, O Lord!
> All mortal wrongs,
> All thoughtless words,
> Crush them, O Lord, with your fury,
> This moment, your eternal day.
> Burn dreams, burn hopes,
> But let this soul
> Rise like a bird
> And wake you with a song.

Silence fell upon the scene once more. Everyone stood where they stood, transfixed. The holy man remained kneeling.

From where we were, Krishna's face looked unmarked and untroubled. It was a tender face. It was almost a child's face. Vikram looked down at the dark strands of hair, loose and dishevelled, and the thick streak of vermillion spread over the parting. It was a beautiful face.

They had dressed Krishna in a white *sari* whose crimson border was soon in ashes. Even the crimson bridal stains on her feet gradually became indistinguishable from the rest of her body. The muddy waters were transformed as they reflected the glory of death. The reflection grew smaller as the pyre caved in and plunged into its own ashes.

A low mist started crawling over the river towards us. It swelled up little by little as the morning drew near. Vikram lifted his head to watch its passage from the west where the moon now stood pale and shrinking.

The kneeling man stood up suddenly. Keeping in step with his jangling chains, he walked over to where Vikram and I waited with the others. "This is where we all stop," he said, looking into Vikram's eyes. "It is I who have led you here. Forgive me if the journey was painful, the company cheerless. But you would have come this way even without me. Time would have brought you here. Time which draws us out of darkness. Time which impales us in its hub. Generous Time which sets us free to wander on its rim. Cruel Time which casts us adrift in the night as it spins along its endless course."

Turning his head to the fire, he said, "Yes, the end is near. Your story, poor girl, is ended. Maybe it seems unfinished. A cruel end. But plots unravel every moment of our lives. Stories begin and end where they will. Some begin while others end.

Some begin before others have ended." The holy man paused and laughed, a sad, hollow laugh.

"What I set out to do was stop the passage of Time. To find time to look behind and look ahead. To look askance. Even to close my eyes and capture the moment. I leave to others the stories that have ended between the beginning and the end of this woman's. Let untold stories rise from your heart so she will live again. Let the story be the teller of the tale."

His dark eyes, reflecting the angry tongues of fire, softened and smiled on us all. "You stand prisoners of my pleasure," he said. "But I can't hold you forever. A moment, a few moments, is all that I have. These I may stir and mix, and pour into vials for you to keep or crush as your fancy wills. What is told cannot be untold. What is written is imperishable. That is why I rejoice as the shadows close in on me, as they will on you. For I have soared into the clouds and lifted the covers of darkness, of things insubstantial."

He paused and turned to the dying fire. "Look what I found," he said, with a flowing gesture of his hand which took in earth, water, the sky, and fire.

He looked curiously at Vikram's face a little longer, ignoring the rest of us. Then he turned round and started walking to the sound of his jangling chains and was swallowed by the shadows under the trees. Nobody knew who he was or where he had come from. I thought I had heard his voice before. I knew I had seen him before.

The bed of fallen leaves encircling us all the way to the water's edge heaved with strange sounds from time to time as the wind poked around, turning the odd leaf all the way on its side, lifting others off the ground. Some of the leaves swirled and danced in the air before they fell, others scattered on the water and floated away or piled up in an oozy mass at the riverbank.

As the fire died down, Vikram moved closer to sit directly in front of the ashes. From time to time, the sounds shook him from his trance, made him look around to see if they were footsteps. But there was nobody. And when he finally traced the sounds to the wind playing in the leaves, he was reminded of the slabs of shale marking the paths in the garden, which, as a child, he delighted in prying loose from the earth and peering into the dark, wet underside in search of bugs and other forms of crawling life. All through the night, this single image of his childhood kept returning to him as he stared into the pile of ashes in front of him and stirred them gently with a broken branch.

An invisible sun was burning into the mist. The mist parted a little, revealing the hazy outline of a little boat gliding slowly over the water. We could see nobody on it, but Vikram thought they were probably hidden in the mist and half-light. Krishna's body had disappeared and it seemed the invisible boatmen were carrying her spirit away. A strange sensation of happiness filled Vikram as he caught sight of the looming sail once more. Then the mist moved in, and the mysterious boat disappeared in silence.

seventeen

A WEEK or so later, while rummaging for something he didn't know what, Vikram stumbled upon Krishna's diary, a small nondescript notebook on the first page of which she had written – 'My Travel Poems, from happier times.' The words were dark, written over and over many times.

REMEMBRANCE
(Beirut, en route to Rome and Boston)

When the last comet streaks into this desert sand,
Ground with the naked bones of pilgrims like me;
When darkness masks the sunset one last time
And time is stilled,
What shall we talk about?

What shall we gain remembering
The sea-breeze pressing on your lips
As we stood on Rue Hasn el Minet,
Watching the bronzed and beautiful
Bounce on trampolines on the Yachting School pier?
What, when Beirut turns to dust?

Shadows pass before my eyes.
Do you remember the blind girl
Hiding behind clouds of cheap perfume,
Working for love on the Via Veneto?
You stared at her, and I wondered.
I wonder where she lies.

Like drums and castanets
Quickening heartbeats close in on us.
Even with the end whispering in my ears
I'll plunge into your peacock eyes,
Dewy eyes of illusion and despair,
And escape this empty shell.

We try but cannot understand
This city, this desert engulfing us.
Pitiless stars stare down;
Like ashen aborigines we shiver,
Blinded by sparks of flint on flint
Under ghostgums on the banks of billabongs.

Through hushed gloom
And the stilled hourglass of the cicada
Perhaps I'll discover you again
Some day.

Some day
When, like a glowing beacon, my wedding ring
Lies buried in untouched seams of anthracite,
While in some rimless valley,
Mingled with pebbles in a nameless stream,
Rolls the gold filling from your punctured molar.

For now,
Silence is all.

AN APOLOGY
(Somewhere in England, or maybe Scotland)

The snow lies huddled over the land today,
Tomorrow it may be gone.
Vague shadows etch the bare trees upon its back.
A cat lies in wait,
While a suburb is hammered in place.
The grass has withered, the leaves are dead,
The fires burn each day.

Smoke from your burning forest
Where earth melts to gold
Stirs the smoke from my burning flesh
And sets me free.

But you my love remain a prisoner
In a prison these hands helped shape,
In a prison I should've smashed,
Walls and pillars and all.

I failed;
Loved this land too late.
Now there's nothing left for you.

STREET SONG
(By a river, somewhere!)

Romance in the sky's not for me,
No adventure in the open road.
The gutter's my home.
Dancing feet before my eyes,
Hems that dare me dream
All day long.
I'm a frog, a worm, a bug;
Come, set me free
Before you're sucked into the red,
Fulfilled by profits of the day.

Do you suppose I'll live through this night
Like last night and the night before?

A mother's haunted eyes
Follow me like an echo,
As I flee a father
Who never was,
To the woman who watched the moon
Slip behind the ships
Glowing in the bay,
Her hand in mine.

The gutter's no place to view the moon.
There are no loaves in the sky tonight.

MEMORIES OF AN URBAN UNIVERSITY
(My only visit to Boston)

Tangled in the towering chimney
The sunlight leans
Into the bowels of academe
And turns pale.

Down below, a forest of Arden
Riddled with decision trees,
A plastic globe
Sick of heart with goals and strategies.

Somewhere there's a Vendler
Resuscitating Yates and Herbert,
But a cold touch of the frenzied world
And the young heart sinks.

So we shuffle along the corridors,
Finger the change in our pockets,
And stare at scribbled odes to devirgination
On one more campus urinal.

The green and orange streetcar
Slithers down the rails,
Shuddering to its own infernal clatter
Below Brookline.

The wind splits the aching seeds

Spilled on the sidewalk,
Breathes brief life into litter
But barely stirs the Charles.

BOAT PEOPLE
(Thinking of Death, along the Seine!)

There was a time when life was small,
Pains chained, desire unburnt.
The secrets I had I shared
With squirrels, crickets, marbles, frogs.
I was one with clouds that roared
Through skies by lightning lit
And, exhausted,
Crashed at the ocean's feet
Beyond Cape Comorin.

My muscles strained and throbbed
As the boatmen's glistening bodies
Bent on splintered tillers and pushed
The aging boats inch by creaking inch.
I slept with ease at the ocean's feet;
I slept with hope and saw the boats
Float like whispers to the sunset,
And heard the swallows panting to the east.

But I sleep no more
For there is no ease nor hope.
The boatmen leave their boats
And beg for coins.
In bubbling bloodied oceans
Little fish dart in and out
Of dead men's eyes,

And snakes that swim
Lie coiled in hollow groins.

DEAD GIRL
(A place I've never been)

The desert crept into my soul before its time
The sand mingled with my blood and wounded flesh
All too soon.
The lightning that tore through the skies
The fire sprouting from the earth
That killed my dreams.
I thought they came from God
Even as my mother sang me to my grave
And my father howled in rage.
The dream was gone
And I knew God was one of us
Mortal like the rest.

A hawk flies across the skies of Tripoli
My spirit rides on its wings.

PRAYER
(Don't remember where)

Parading images drag
Their tired feet across the page;
I read in their stares
The sadness of my age.

I once saw a lonely man
Straddling the grass
By the road to the Cape;
His lips kissed a bamboo flute,
The notes vaulted over the twisted brush
Like a muezzin's evening call
Or a Brahmin's hymn to Ganga at dawn.

I've sat perspiring under peepul trees,
Plotting the sun's unwavering fixity
Against my slipshod life.
But I'm no *avatar*
And *nirvana* never rained on me.

Now the notes haunt me
Across the pitch pines and bayberries,
Cradling my loneliness
Like a lotus in a vast unwrinkled sea,
Shadowless and unshadowed.

I remember a park-bench conversation

I once overheard.
Mother was ninety three last week, she said,
Wanted to play the piano.
So they wheeled her down to the lounge
Where she struck one key,
One single note,
And murmured, "Pretty."

I'm starting to believe in
Shadows cast by torn butterfly wings,
In the empty mermaid's purse,
Invisible crow's feet creeping on my face.
Seems there's an eye
Watching me over the river's edge,
Fixing its beam as if on a straw,
Pushing it through the whirlpool's cone.
I'm beginning to believe
In the emptiness tightening round us
Little by little each day.

Suddenly I can see
My silver eyes unblinking
After the millionth time
In a blackened skillet
Swallowing all reflection.

I hoped to carry with me, to my end,
Secret whispers and conceptual echoes
Of unpremeditated summer nights

Sharpening fury and desire
Upon a shaft of steel,
Bridging with the frailest ties
One unknown with another.

How will it end?
Where will it end?

Don't tell me the price the pay
Is a measure of what we learn.
If only I could see my God
I'd consume in a single prayer
Flashing moments I thought I lived
And watch my empty visions burn.

And the hibiscus tree bloomed massive yellow flowers month after month, year after year............

THE END